SAVING HER COWBOY

BROTHERS OF MILLER RANCH BOOK TWO

NATALIE DEAN

OTHER BOOKS BY NATALIE DEAN

CONTEMPORARY ROMANCE

Miller Family Saga

BROTHERS OF MILLER RANCH

Miller Family Saga Series 1

Her Second Chance Cowboy

Saving Her Cowboy

Her Rival Cowboy

Her Fake-Fiance Cowboy Protector

Taming Her Cowboy Billionaire

Brothers of Miller Ranch Complete Collection

MILLER BROTHERS OF TEXAS

Miller Family Saga Series 2

The New Cowboy at Miller Ranch Prologue

Humbling Her Cowboy

In Debt to the Cowboy

The Cowboy Falls for the Veterinarian

Almost Fired by the Cowboy

Faking a Date with Her Cowboy Boss

Miller Brothers of Texas Complete Collection

BRIDES OF MILLER RANCH, N.M.

Miller Family Saga Series 3

Cowgirl Fallin' for the Single Dad

Cowgirl Fallin' for the Ranch Hand

Cowgirl Fallin' for the Neighbor

Cowgirl Fallin' for the Miller Brother

Cowgirl Fallin' for Her Best Friend's Brother

Cowboy Fallin' in Love Again

Brides of Miller Ranch Complete Collection

Miller Family Wrap-up Story

(An update on all your favorite characters!)

Copper Creek Romances

BAKER BROTHERS OF COPPER CREEK

Copper Creek Romances Series 1

Cowboys & Protective Ways

Cowboys & Crushes

Cowboys & Christmas Kisses

Cowboys & Broken Hearts

Cowboys & Second Chances

Cowboys & Wedding Woes

Cowboys' Mom Finds Love

Baker Brothers of Copper Creek Complete Collection

<u>**CALLAHANS OF COPPER CREEK**</u>

Copper Creek Romances Series 2

Making a Cowgirl

Marrying a Cowgirl

Christmas with a Cowgirl

Trusting a Cowgirl

Dating a Cowgirl

Catching a Cowgirl

Loving a Cowgirl

Marrying a Cowboy

Callahans of Copper Creek Complete Collection

<u>**KEAGANS OF COPPER CREEK**</u>

Copper Creek Romances Series 3

Some Cowboys are Off-Limits

Some Cowgirls Love Single Dads

Some Cowboys are Infuriating

Some Cowboys Don't Like City Girls

Some Cowboys Heal Broken Hearts

Some Cowboys are Just Friends (Coming July 2024)

Though I try to keep this list updated in each book, you may also visit my website nataliedeanauthor.com for the most up to date information on my book list.

1

Missy

issy held her chin high, hazel eyes locked on a certain point just in front of her. She could feel a couple of sidelong glances, some of them reproachful, some of them appreciative, but she ignored them. Just like she'd been doing for years.

At least the weather was nice on her walk to the town's grocery. Lately, the summer wind had decided to take a vacation, leaving the town sweltering in its own heat. But finally, the breeze was back, caressing her spine and wicking the sweat away from her brow.

Checking herself in the window before she entered the store, Missy made sure she didn't look a mess. Her blond hair was pulled back into a neat and sensible ponytail. She was wearing a simple button-down blouse instead of the tank top she normally sported, and her jeans were crisp, newly washed at the town's only small laundromat.

Wiping her palms on her jeans and willing them not to be sweaty in case she needed to shake someone's hand, Missy strolled inside.

She looked around for a moment, unsure who she should talk to. There were no managers in sight and only one cashier on duty. Strange, for it being summer. Normally, this was when they hired several high school students to work around the place.

Maybe they were on the afternoon shift, and the morning was left to the veterans. That would make sense. Nodding to herself, Missy headed over to the woman with a polite smile on her face.

"Hi, my name's Melissa Dominic, I'm here to inquire about a resumé I sent in?"

The woman looked up from the notebook she had in front of her, and Missy knew instantly that her expression wasn't a welcoming one.

The cashier looked to be only a few years older than Missy, with chestnut hair up in a tight bun. She was largely unremarkable, but the derisive look in her eyes was certainly stinging.

"I know who you are. You're Vinnie's daughter."

Oh. Well, that was unfortunate.

It had been three years since her father had passed away, yet she was still known as the daughter of the town drunk. She knew that reputations liked to stick in smalls towns, but it wasn't like he had been that way since she had been born.

No, once he had been a functioning member of society. But then he'd had to watch his wife succumb to an incredibly painful death thanks to ovarian cancer. After that, the bottle had offered him a comfort the rest of the world didn't have.

It only took seven years for him to cement his reputation, and even three years after his liver gave up, it was like he had never left. People still presumed things about Missy. They still remembered his every slurred declaration and drunken mistake like it was yesterday.

Sometimes, it felt like she was never going to escape his stumbling shadow.

"Ah, were you friends with him?"

The woman snorted. "Hardly."

It probably would have been too much to ask that she was. Still, Missy shook off the shock and plowed forward. Her mother had always told her that she was too tenacious for her own good, and that certainly hadn't changed in the ten years since her passing.

"I see. Anyway, about my resumé—"

"Let me stop you right there," the cashier said, the look in her eyes growing even more condescending. "The owners aren't going to like you, and whoever took your application seemed to know that because nothing's been submitted to them in weeks."

Missy drew herself up to her full height, letting her form tense. It wasn't that she slouched around, but she did often find herself subconsciously trying to make herself smaller. Less... conspicuous. However, this moment seemed like the perfect time to use all of her five feet, ten inches.

The woman did indeed seem to shrink back just a bit, the shadow of Missy's shoulders cutting off some of the light from the window. When Missy was younger, she had hated how she was always growing, always gaining weight, always getting bigger and bigger than the other girls. But now she found it suited her.

Somewhere between chubby and jacked, she usually felt a

bit like an Amazon. Sure, it hurt when she banged her wide hips into a kitchen counter and finding bras to fit her sizable chest was possibly the most annoying thing in existence, but when she looked in the mirror, she finally felt satisfied. There was a power to her form. A softness that spoke of her femininity, but a hardness that said she wasn't someone to mess around with.

That second part was what she wanted the cashier to focus on.

"I'm afraid I don't catch your meaning," Missy said, saccharinely sweet.

Missy certainly didn't mean the cashier any violence, but she didn't need to know that.

The cashier licked her lips, eyes darting around nervously before answering. "You know what I mean."

"I'm afraid I don't. Would I be able to fill out an application with you?"

"I-I..."

Just when it seemed the woman was going to cave, an elderly patron pushed up a loaded shopping cart. That extra bit of company seemed to bolster the store clerk because her expression hardened.

"Look, you're not a good fit here, and we both know it. You should check out the bar. Plenty of them knew your father, and I'm sure you'd fit in fine behind the counter."

Missy's cheeks burned. True, while she could probably go there, she didn't want to be within a mile of alcohol if she could help it. But she wasn't going to let this woman insult her in front of anyone, even if it was just a kind-looking old lady.

"I'm curious why you think I wouldn't be a good fit. You said yourself that you haven't seen my application, so it can't be a lack of skills." Missy tilted her head, thinking. "So, what is it?

You're worried that I might be a bit too much like my drunk of a father? Or by not fitting in, do you mean that I might actually fill out the uniform a little too well?"

Missy was well aware of the assumptions people made when they took in her figure. Although apparently being 'thick' was in lately, people certainly liked to let their imaginations run wild when they took in her hourglass figure. When she was younger, Missy would try to smother herself in layers and layers of clothes. But now that she was older, she dressed for the weather. If other people stared, that was their problem, not hers. When it was hot outside, she was going to wear her shorts and tank tops just like anyone else might do.

Whatever confidence she had gotten from the old lady faded as another family came up, this time a woman who was trying to wrangle what looked like twins. "It's just—I..."

Although Missy enjoyed the cashier's withering attitude, she knew that there wasn't any winning this situation. Even if the woman did take Missy's application, the cashier would probably just toss it the moment she left. Oh well. It wasn't like this was the last option.

"It's all right. I think I catch your drift. You have a good day now."

Missy tipped her head and spun on her heel, heading toward the door. She kept her head up and her shoulders broadened all the way out the entrance, and she didn't allow herself to slump until she was out of sight.

Ugh.

It wouldn't do good to get upset in public, so Missy busied herself with grabbing one of the classifieds and opening it for a moment. She didn't read any of the words, but it was giving her a couple of seconds to conceal her watery eyes.

Ever since she was young, she'd had the annoying reflex of crying whenever she was angry. It was a hot, prickly sort of tearing up that made her feel even more embarrassed than the act of getting angry did. She hated it because people thought they were hurting her feelings when in reality, they were making her burn with rage. Granted, it didn't happen very often now that she was out of high school, but every now and then, things got to her.

"Excuse me, miss?"

Missy took a deep breath through her nose and lowered her paper to see the little old lady from inside. Great. Was she here to drive in the point that the cashier had been trying to get across?

"Yes, ma'am?"

"I hope you don't mind, but I couldn't help but overhear your conversation—" Yeah, that much was obvious. Her whole presence was why the cashier had gotten a second wind in the first place. "Are you looking for work, young lady?"

Missy nodded, tucking her newspaper under her arm. Normally she was quite on guard with strangers, but there was something disarming about the unassuming woman.

She was short and tanned, with grey hair that was in a long braid at the nape of her neck. She had green eyes that looked quite discerning, but not in a mean way. More of a wise way.

"Yes, I am."

"Are you new to town?"

"No, I've lived here since I was three." The woman looked like she was expecting more explanation, and for some reason, Missy found herself indulging her. "I was working for the vet the next town over, cleaning cages, running the front desk and doing all of that stuff that didn't require a vet degree, but he decided to retire and take care of his wife after she had a stroke."

"Oh goodness, well I'm glad he was there for her. Did he not sell the business?"

"He did, but the buyer basically has his whole family working for him, so they didn't need me at all."

"I suppose that I can't blame him, but that certainly is a bummer." The woman paused for a moment, regarding Missy, and for once she didn't feel like she was being judged. "You know, if you're looking for work, I have a bit of a farm outside of town, and I could use a muckraker for the stalls. Usually, my boys take care of it. But three of them left to prep for their first year of college, so we're short this summer.

The woman wiped her brow with a handkerchief, then continued.

"It's hard work, but it's honest, and you look strong enough to handle it."

Huh. Missy didn't think anyone had ever complimented her on looking strong, and she found she liked it a lot more than people commenting on her curves. "Are you serious?"

The woman nodded, a small smile around her mouth. "I wouldn't joke about something like a job in this economy. If you're game to try, I'm game to let you."

Missy couldn't believe her luck. After a whole lot of storm clouds, it seemed like the sky was finally clearing. "Yeah! Of course. I would love that."

"Perfect!" The woman pulled a tiny notebook from her purse and quickly jotted something down. She ripped off the small sheet with a flourish and handed it to Missy. "It's a Thursday now, so why don't you come on down Monday? We normally pay cash once per week, but if you're a little strapped at the moment, I don't mind starting my workers on paying them daily for a bit."

"Wait, really?" Missy's eyes widened. She'd been budgeting like a champ since she had found out she was losing her job. *And* she'd been looking for work, but she was down to her last couple hundred. It sure would be nice to have something to eat other than rice and beans or mac n' cheese and tuna.

"Honey, I know how hard it can be in today's day and age. Often it seems like the rich are getting richer while the poor are getting poorer. We do what we can but..." She shrugged a bit. "Let's not prattle on about that. I'll see you Monday?"

"Yes, you will!" Missy answered happily.

A blue, extended cab pick-up pulled up, one that Missy could tell was expensive, and the woman ambled up to it. An older man came out of the driver's seat and helped load the groceries into the back, his lean arms layered with decades of muscles and veins. Missy offered to help—the least she could do considering she had just been given a job—but he just waved her off and bid her a good day.

Missy lingered for a moment before deciding to respect his decision and wandered off toward her apartment. It wasn't until she was near her place that she looked down at the piece of paper that she was holding so incredibly tightly.

The words took a moment to make out considering the bright sun overhead, but as soon as she could read them, a jolt went down her spine. She knew this address. Just as everyone else in town did.

Somehow, without even trying, she had gotten a job at the *Miller Ranch*.

Missy stared down at the small scrap of paper, her breath catching. The Miller Ranch was a staple of the town, been there since before the state was even a state. And the family that ran it was *incredibly* wealthy. Like... Missy had heard they were up in the billions. And all from treating their animals with respect instead of going grand scale.

She couldn't believe it!

After so many months of looking, a job had just landed in her lap!

She just hoped it went well. If there was something that she had learned in her years of being a ne'er-do-well of the town, it was that the well-off people were all too happy to remind those under them exactly of their position.

Oh well, she wasn't about to look a gift horse in the mouth.

Especially not a gift horse that paid in cash.

2

———————

Bart

*E*xplosions.

Dirt flew everywhere, particulates hitting the sides of the armored vehicle, his helmet, his goggles. Everything was enveloped in a cacophony of death and destruction, but Bart couldn't turn his head one way or the other.

"Help me!"

"God, my arm!"

"Move!"

Too many screams to comprehend, the occasional one lurching through the maelstrom but most of them blending into a constant shriek of terror. The telltale staccato of gunfire provided a rhythm to the symphony of horror around him, driving his heart into a harder and harder tempo.

Then, just above, a sound he knew all too well. It was a distinctive whistle, one that only came before something even more devastating.

No.

He wasn't going to lose more of his friends to RPGs.

As if darkness had been lifted from beside him, he saw his best squadmate curled on the ground, holding his bleeding face. Diving over him, Bart protected him from the blast as best he could.

Except instead of hitting the hard-packed earth of the desert, he landed in a relatively soft pile of hay.

Oh.

That wasn't right.

Vision slowly clearing, Bart tried not to succumb to the intense nausea rolling through him. As usual, it took him several minutes to get right in his body and mind without feeling like tossing his cookies.

He laid there, breathing like his therapist taught him, and eventually, he felt tethered to reality enough to open his eyes. Glancing around, he realized that he was back home. He was safe.

There were no missiles.

There was no blood.

It was just him, a bucket of paint, and a couple of animals.

Sighing to himself, Bart stood. He was glad that none of his family was around to see his embarrassing display. As far as they knew, his episodes were getting fewer and farther in-between. Bart would prefer if they stayed believing that. Because if they knew that it felt like not much had changed to him, then maybe they might lose all hope.

Goodness knew he was almost there himself. Something was broken in him, and he had the feeling it wasn't fixable.

Bart shook his head. This was no time to be melancholy.

Besides, the more he let his thoughts linger on the darkness that liked to brew in his skull, the more likely he was to slip off into...

Into memories he'd rather not revisit.

A quick scan of the ground revealed that he had dropped his paintbrush on the hay. Oh right. As a surprise, he had been painting some of the stalls of the barn that his brothers were renovating. Ben had left during the weekend on a trip with his relatively new girlfriend Chastity, while Benji was helping with a cattle drive. He'd thought that this would have been a pleasant treat for the third of the barn that they had finished, but it wouldn't be if he spilled paint everywhere.

His eyes slid to the upended can, and he sighed once more. "Guess I better clean that up before it dries," he murmured, going over to one of the wash-sinks and attaching a strong hose.

Thankfully, it didn't take long to wash away the mess and put away the rest of his supplies. He would try again another day. As usual, he was incredibly tired after one of his episodes and just wanted to lay down.

To think that he had once been an endless ball of energy. Those times seemed so far behind now, back when he was a young prankster and the life of every party. Almost like a different lifetime.

He wished that he had gone to college or even stayed at the ranch like Ben. But no, he'd had adventure and patriotism in his blood, so he'd gone and ran off to—

"Hey, what's going on in here?"

Bart whirled to look at his brother Bradley. He was shocked to see his younger brother, who had been backpacking across Europe for the past four months. He had arrived a couple of days back, but Bart had kind of forgotten about it completely. Sometimes, his memory wasn't the greatest. It seemed that little details would slip away from him, vanishing into the ether where the rest of those lost moments went.

"Just painting."

"Cool. You want a hand?"

Bart bristled. "I can paint by myself. I don't need a babysitter."

"I'm not saying you do," Bradley retorted easily. He was always so even-tempered. "But I was always the artistic one in the family, so I thought I might be able to lend a hand. You know, since I've basically got nothing else to do until Ben and Benji get back."

Bart relaxed for a moment, telling himself he needed to chill. His brothers had always been there for him. There was no need to snap at him.

"If you want to grab another can, we can finish up this chunk together."

"Right on. In the maintenance shed, right?"

"Yeah."

Bart collected himself as his brother walked off and by the time Bradley was back, he felt much more in check.

They got to work quickly, and the painting was fairly relaxing. Almost like before he had gone off—before his world had crumbled around him. Before he was some sort of charity case taken on by his family instead of *being* part of the family.

"I miss this smell," Bradley said with a sigh, a wan smile on his face.

Bart just snorted. "Which smell? The paint? The crap? The animals?"

"All of it." Bradley laughed. "Even the bad stuff. Don't get me wrong, the air in Europe was great, but there's nothing like the ranch.

"Also, I definitely got soft while I was wandering around. Even backpacking, scuba diving, and hiking don't compare to a summer's worth of ranch work."

Bart shared a laugh with him on that. "I know what you mean. For a bit, basic training was like a break to me. But then they caught on and singled me out for more personalized exercises."

"It's because you were bragging, weren't you?"

Bart smirked. "You know me so well."

"Yeah, I'd like to think so. You're only the second oldest brother in our little dynasty."

"Dynasty?" Bart snorted. "I wouldn't call us that."

"Really? You wouldn't? We only happen to be a wealthy family that's kept all our resources in our bloodline for generations and has no plans of changing that anytime soon."

"Well, when you put it like that..."

The conversation went on from there, with lulls and peaks, and plenty of comfortable silence. It almost made Bart feel normal, if that were possible.

They had finished all of one side when it was beginning to grow dark. Which meant that they either missed dinner or it was about to be called. Bart stretched, setting his stuff in the sink.

"I think I'm gonna head back to the house," he said, turning on the water.

"Yeah, it's about time. You want me to walk you back?"

Bart bristled, his teeth going on edge. It felt infantilizing to be constantly monitored, and he didn't need it.

But as he stepped out into the night air, he felt dizziness swamp him, a sort of slipping feeling like he wasn't where he was supposed to be. Reality had a strange sort of soapiness to it, threatening to slip out of his grip entirely.

"Bart? You want some company?" Bradley asked his brother again.

"Yeah, that would be nice," he murmured, tucking his pride away. His therapist had told him time and time again that his illness was something akin to a broken leg. If his limb was in a cast, he wouldn't keep walking on it, so since his mind had the injury, he needed to take care of it.

His brother finished up washing his brush and closing the paint can then joined Bart. Together they headed toward the main house. He was pretty sure that a warm meal would do him good.

If there was one thing that could tether him to the real world, it was Ma's cooking. Nothing like a full belly to keep him rooted. At the moment, it was the best anchor he had.

3

———

Missy

$\mathcal{M}$issy drove past the Miller Ranch sign, still hardly believing that it was all real. She kept wondering if she had just dreamed the whole thing up and was about to make a fool of herself. But she supposed she couldn't turn back now, especially with a whole job on the line.

The long, *long* drive eventually lead her up to a large, beautifully constructed cabin. It was at least three stories with a wraparound porch and large bay windows that no doubt let in tons of light. There was a massive garden outside, with flowers of every kind and thick ivy climbing up the sunny side of the house.

"Wow," she murmured to herself, throwing the car into park and turning the engine off.

She sat there for a moment, not sure where to go, when a young man sauntered up to her car.

He was tall with sandy brown hair and hazel eyes. He had a scar across his chin but was handsome, in a roguish sort of way. He seemed to be around her age, but she didn't remember him in any of her classes. And considering her graduating class was only 87 students, there was no way she would have forgotten him.

"Hey there! You must be the new hire around here. I'm Bradley Miller. Ma said you'd been coming in today."

"Yeah, that's me," Missy answered, feeling relieved. "Melissa Dominic, but you can call me Missy."

"All right then, Missy. If you want to turn your car back on, I'll walk ya to where you're gonna park from now on."

"Sounds like a plan."

She did as he said, and he walked her around the back of the house and down a small path to a bit of a dirt lot where there were several other cars. Not nearly enough for all the workers that had to be on the ranch, but she vaguely knew that a lot of the employees lived on Miller land, something about them being distant family members or cousins or something.

Once she was parked, she stepped out to receive a hearty handshake from the gentleman. Despite his young age, he didn't look her up or down, or have his eyes linger where they shouldn't. Instead, those hazel eyes stayed on her face, a pleasant grin on his own.

It was too soon to say, but Missy was beginning to be a bit hopeful about this whole Miller family business.

"All right, you ready to do a bit of a walkabout?"

Missy nodded, nerves bubbling in her stomach. She kept waiting for something bad to happen, like some sort of *Aha!* moment where something terrible occurred. Because that was her luck and always had been. If there was one thing that the Dominics never had, it was luck.

"So, you're mostly going to be working in the main barn. The ranch hands will be letting out the animals in shifts, with the cows staying out most of the day, the sheep staying out for three or four hours twice a day, as long as the weather is nice, and the pigs out for about half the day. You have to be careful with them, you know, as they can get overheated real quick."

"What about predators?" Missy asked, seeing the large building loom into view over a hill.

"Well, we have pretty nice pens for that reason. And then there's the dogs."

"The dogs?"

"Yeah, we've got Ivan, Chester, and Fargo who roam and make sure everything's all right. They've chased off coyotes and thieves alike.

"Then there's our sheepdogs, Cookie, Ophelia, Maggie, and Dunkirk. They protect the sheep, herd them, make sure they don't wander off. They only come in when they want, while Chester and Fargo are generally inside every night."

"Wow. Sounds like a real pack."

"Yeah, you'll meet them. They're real friendly. And then there's the cats."

"What, you have guard cats or something?" Missy laughed.

"Actually, you could say that." Bradley chuckled. "They keep out the rats and mice from the barns, and we just so happened to have a Maine Coon tomcat wander here when I was a kid, so now we've got some real monsters running around. I've seen a couple of them chase off a few coyotes, they're that tough."

"I have a hard time believing that—"

As if on cue, a fence came into view with a large shape sitting on one of the posts. For a moment, Missy didn't recognize it, but as they approached, she realized it was indeed one of the largest cats she had ever seen.

It was gray and black but thickly coated like some sort of ancient, regal beast. Its head was nearly the size of a dog's, and its tail was beautifully thick with fur that looked more like a feathered plume than something belonging to a cat. Missy reckoned the thing had to be near twenty pounds, and it wasn't even fat by any means.

"Wow. You weren't kidding."

"What? You mean Bitsy here? She was the runt of her litter, actually. She's kind of our baby. Probably why she's the friendliest out of all of them."

"Word of advice, if you see one of the cats, let them come to you rather than vice versa. They're nice but—well, you know how cats are."

"Don't worry. I'm good with animals."

"Are ya?"

Missy nodded her head, pausing as they passed by the cat to offer her hand. She made sure not to come from above, but rather slightly below the cat's noble head, and she stopped a bit away from it, laying her palm flat.

Bitsy regarded her for a moment, as if she was thinking, then carefully sniffed at Missy's hand with her dark nose. After a few moments of inspection, she let out a tiny chirp and pushed her amazingly soft and furred head into Missy's palm.

"There ya go. You're a sweet thing, aren't you?"

"Well isn't that something? Bitsy is friendly, but normally she's a bit more cautious around strangers."

"Like I said, I do well with animals."

"That's gonna do you great here, that's for sure. The cows are a whole lot easier to work with if they like you. We once had a muckraker who gave them the stink eye when they first joined us, and I'd never seen a single worker get projectile cow-pied so many times in one month. They ran 'em right off the ranch."

Missy paled slightly. "Did you say *projectile* cow pies?"

"Oh, don't worry about that. It doesn't happen very often unless a cow is sick or startled, and usually, it's us ranch hands who get that treatment. As a muckraker, you just gotta watch your step."

"If you say so…"

Thankfully the conversation shifted away from cow pies as they reached the main barn. Or at least, Missy assumed it was the main barn given its size and impressive structure. The thing was twice as big as the main house she had passed, and it was painted a beautiful shade of deep blue.

"I'm supposed to clean this every day?" Missy's eyes were wide. She didn't even know how that was possible.

"Hardly!" Bradley laughed beside her. "There's five of you who work in here, and generally, the goal is three stalls an hour. Altogether, it'll take about a week for your group to get through the whole barn. Then you start right back over again."

"That's a relief." Missy pretended like she was wiping sweat from her forehead, making a joke out of her lack of knowledge about life on the farm.

"There are plenty of other little chores as well to keep you occupied, just things that come up here or there. And of course, you get an hour and a half lunch and several breaks."

"An hour and a half lunch?"

"Yeah, you can't exactly run to the store or for fast food around here, so ya either eat in the worker's cabin or back at your house. People need travel time, ya know?"

"How do you get anything done?" Missy felt like she was asking a lot of questions, but Bradley was still smiling and seemed to enjoy talking about the farm.

"Well, we start at five thirty in the morning generally. Speaking of which, Ma said she never told you our hours. Does six to three thirty sound doable to you?" Bradley raised his eyebrows as he looked at her.

"Yes. It'll be a little rough for a bit since I'm used to sleeping in, but I did it for high school. I can certainly do it for this."

"All right, that's what I like to hear. That can-do attitude will do you well. Now, let's get into what you'll be doing here on the ranch..."

He started listing off her responsibilities, going through a stall and showing her step by step how to take care of it. She noticed that there were others in the background also working, and Bradley assured her they would be around if she had any questions.

By the time he finished, they were at least two hours into her first day. She was eager to get started. Sure, the barn smelled like poop, hay, and animals, and sure, she knew her whole body was gonna hurt real bad for a good while, but she was happiest being productive.

Laziness made her feel like she was proving everyone right —like she really wasn't ever going to be good for anything.

Shaking that thought out of her head, she beamed as Bradley gave her a pitchfork. "So, you think you're ready for me to let you tackle a stall on your own? To be honest, I just got back from a really long trip myself, and I've got a whole ton to catch up on."

Missy nodded happily. It was happening. She really had a job! But there were a couple of details that she was still missing.

"Um, Mr. Miller?"

"Bradley, please. My Pa's Mr. Miller and even he doesn't like being called that."

"All right. Bradley, am I working full time or part time around here?"

"Geez, Ma didn't tell you anything, did she?"

Missy shrugged. "She told me she had a job for me to do, and I showed up. That was all I needed to know at first."

"Hah! That's true. Yeah, it's full time. And you can pitch in some overtime every now and then if Ben approves it."

"Ben?"

"He's the oldest brother and in charge of most of that stuff. I'm just taking care of things while he's out with his new lady."

"Ah. I see. And is it..."

"Time and a half? Yeah." Bradley's eyes crinkled mischievously. "It'd be mighty awful of us to do as well as we do and not take care of our workers appropriately."

"Awful, but still pretty common nowadays. And, if you don't mind me asking, what exactly... is the wage to start off with?" Missy wasn't expecting anything more than minimum wage, but she was worried that maybe there was some sort of cheaper day laborer rate or something that was going on. Since she had been promised to be paid in cash, and she hadn't even signed any paperwork yet.

"We start ya off with fifteen dollars an hour around here. After six months, if you're doing well, we give ya a dollar raise. After that, we do a yearly review where you're guaranteed at least a quarter raise."

Missy's eyes widened. "*Fifteen dollars an hour?*"

Sure, while she knew that was the going rate in New York and other big cities, that was a huge amount for her small town.

Most people she knew were living pretty comfortably at twelve dollars an hour. She couldn't imagine...

Wow. Her life was certainly about to change.

"We have health insurance and all that too. But I hope you don't mind, I don't wanna touch that stuff with a ten-foot pole. We'll get ya rolling on that front when my brother comes back to town. Sound good?"

Missy nodded eagerly. "It certainly does! Thank you."

"No problem! I'll roll around later to check up on you."

He walked off as if he hadn't just completely rocked Missy's budgetary world, leaving the young woman to stare over the stalls that were supposed to be her duty.

Fifteen dollars an hour.

Holy smokes.

Well, she needed to get to work if she was going to be earning *that* kind of rate.

"Oh, wow, hey there, don't push yourself so hard on the first day."

Missy blinked and turned around to see Bradley standing there with his arms crossed over his chest. For a split second, her heart leapt into her throat, sure that he was coming to tell her that they had heard about her reputation and didn't need that on the ranch. That she didn't *belong*.

But instead, a smile broke across his face as he whistled. "Geez, if you work this hard every day, maybe we won't need overtime."

Missy grinned weakly, trying to wipe off her sweaty forehead with the back of her hand, but as she did, she could feel something smear across her skin. Considering what she had been cleaning for the past... however long, she didn't want to think about what it could be.

"I doubt that. I'm sure I'll be nice and sore tomorrow."

"Yes, that is typically how bodies work." He laughed slightly, all the way to his eyes, and she understood why the girls in town got so giggly over the Miller boys. "So please, feel free to slow your roll for the rest of the day."

"I'll take that into consideration." She looked him over once more, and when he didn't leave, her curiosity piqued. "Did you need something else? Me to sign something?"

"Nah, it's just lunch time, and I figure you should be shown to where a lot of the workers eat. Unless you want to drive home."

"Oh, is it lunch already?"

"Technically, it started a bit ago, but I figured since you weren't here from our normal start time that you wouldn't be hungry yet."

"You guessed right," Missy said, setting her pitchfork aside. "But I sure am hungry now."

"Yeah, if I knew you were going to go after this like a rabbit with a carrot, I'd have gotten you earlier."

"Well, I guess you and me both learned something today." Missy had stepped over to the sink and wiped her forehead and washed her hands.

"I guess so." He stepped aside for her to pass him, which she did until they were out of the barn, then he took over the lead. "I see those muscles aren't just for show."

With that Missy gave him a bit of a smirk. "Us Dominics are hardy stock. Dad used to joke that we've been the bodyguards of many an important man throughout the centuries."

"Huh, aren't you in the wrong line of business then? I hear bodyguards pay a whole lot more than farmhands."

Missy shrugged. "I don't really like hurting things."

"Fair enough."

They came upon a neat looking shack; the door was thrown open and pleasant conversation could be heard from within. Missy followed Bradley inside and was surprised to see a large, doublewide table with over a dozen people sitting around it, stuffing their faces. Over against the wall was another long bar that was filled up with all sorts of food, bolstering fare that would give her enough energy to get through the day.

"Hello everyone, this is Missy," Bradley said with a winning smile. A chorus of "hellos" came from the workers at the table.

Bradley turned back toward Missy. "Lunch is normally from eleven to one, and I figured since you're a townie, you'll probably stick around here."

"Yeah, I would hate to drive back and forth," Missy said, feeling self-consciousness prickling up her spine. With so many eyes turned toward her, she couldn't figure out if anyone knew her. Or rather, knew *of* her.

No one in town really knew her that well. There were just words about her father, about her *body*—like she could help that, or *worse*, about her mother.

Mrs. Chelsea Dominic was a wonderful woman. Kind to a fault. Incredibly sarcastic. Missy remembered how her mother taught her that she could do anything. That she was unstoppable. That there was nothing wrong with loving all the strange creatures she loved. Snakes, rats, mice, even worms. Mom had taught her that it was the *life* in them that was so precious. That it didn't matter that their outsides were scaled, or slimy, or covered with matted fur. That they were just as worthy of love as anything else.

"Nice to meet you, Missy," one of the closer men said, a guy who looked to be middle-aged with salt and pepper hair. "Name's Clint."

"Nice to meet you, Clint," she responded automatically, offering her hand.

He took it, and there were no looks of derision, not huffs or knowing glances. That seemed good. Usually, people couldn't hide it on their faces when they thought those ugly, judgy things.

The darkness—the vile, stinking tint of it—always shone through those fake, pleasant masks that they wore.

"Here," another woman said, tall and stocky not unlike Missy herself. "Name's Janey. I'll show you all the best food that Mrs. Miller and Tatum cooks us."

"Thank you," Missy said, eyes widening. "That brings up a couple questions. Question one, who's Tatum?"

"Oh, one of the nieces descended from one of the Miller branching lines. Your other question?"

"Mrs. Miller, as in *the* Mrs. Miller cooks for us?"

Janey chuckled lightly. "Why do people always sound so surprised about that? Yeah, she cooks for us. Not every day, mind you, but most of them."

"Huh," Missy said. She didn't know what to think of that. But it was a good sign, she thought. One of many.

She hoped that it all wasn't too good to be true.

"All right, now that we've got all that out of the way, let's get you some grub, right?"

Missy nodded and followed Janey as she led her along the buffet table. Soon, Missy's plate was full, and she sat down with the others, several of whom kept up polite conversation with her.

It was nice. All of it. For once, she felt that she wasn't being judged. She was just another worker with growing blisters on her newly worked hands. It was nice. Very nice.

She could get used to it.

The only question remaining was just what was going to come along and ruin it like life always did.

4

Missy

"Hey there, Sterling. *Ow,* don't lick Mommy's hand now, she's got icky medical stuff on it."

But the sweet little brown eyes didn't even flick up to her as the sweetest of her little rats licked her fingers. Missy pulled her hand away and patted his head before filling up the food bowl he shared with his brothers.

People always hated rats, said they gave them the creepy-crawlies, but Missy understood what it was like to be judged just on appearances. They were clean little things, and incredibly affectionate. Sterling was an excellent fetcher while Salvatore, his black and white brother, was better at rolling over and playing dead.

Washing her hands once more, wincing as her blisters stung, Missy moved onto her hamsters. Those were mostly from people who bought them for their children then quickly gave them up when they realized how much work the little creatures were. That their cages were too small, and the animals were getting aggressive from pent-up energy.

She laughed as she put one of her three into an exercise ball, then sealed it up properly so Iggy could roll around her studio. Considering that hamsters couldn't be kept together unless they were birth-siblings of the same sex, they took up a lot of her space. She had a tank for each of them with plenty of the stuff they needed to dig and have fulfilling lives with.

But as she loaded Sabby into the next exercise ball, she felt her back throb a bit, sore and abused from her first full week of work.

Not that she was surprised because *boy,* the work was indeed backbreaking. Her hands were covered in blisters and band-aids while she had some serious rub-rash going on between her thick thighs. It seemed that no amount of baby powder was getting her jeans to stop chafing her, so she was probably going to have to invest in some thick leggings that would stand up to the job.

Maybe she'd ask Janey. While the woman wasn't as curvy as Missy, she was still somewhat thick, and no doubt had to find solutions to the dreaded swamp-thighs. Missy resolved to ask the farmhand on Monday, then went about cleaning cages.

It was a relief to not have to worry about her coworkers or shady glances. Although there were dozens of them, none of the farmworkers ever gave her trouble. They were all friendly and never made comments about her body—other than to compliment her growing biceps or tell her remedies for her hands.

But perhaps, best of all, no one ever told her to smile.
She liked that.
She liked that a lot.

Almost as much as she liked all of the animals. There were just *so* many! There were all the sheep, with an especially mischievous one named Blarney. They were dumb creatures, but fun nonetheless, and she liked their personalities.

Then, of course, there were the cows too. While they were usually off grazing in the fields or having fun with their cow-friends, they did occasionally wander in to check on the workers. Or at least Missy liked to think that was what they were doing. Their big eyes were so kind, so curious that she couldn't help but attribute some human characteristics to them.

There were also the ducks, and the geese, and everything else. It was the best job that she had ever worked, even if she woke up sore every morning and hit her bed every night utterly exhausted.

Missy puttered around most of the day, taking care of her animals and cleaning the whole house. It was strangely relaxing, but by the time night finally rolled around, she found she wasn't tired at all.

Huh. It seemed that her body was so used to pushing and pushing itself that having a day off felt strange. Missy drew herself a bath, settling in for a good soak, and it helped wick away some of the soreness in her back, hips, and shoulders.

But when she got out and dried herself, she found that she still wasn't even remotely tired. The town was strangely quiet outside her door, with no lowing of the cows or honking of geese or any other sounds beyond the occasional car.

Sighing, Missy went to the window, opening it up to look at the sky.

Normally there was a great smattering of stars up in the velvet black, blinking softly at her, but with every year they got a little dimmer—drowned out by the light pollution of their growing town. It wouldn't be too long before their small town turned into a fringe city. And then a real city.

Sometimes, Missy thought she would be better off in a bigger city, where nobody knew her, and her father's reputation wouldn't be a thing at all. There would be far too many souls and shakers for someone like her to even make a splash. She could blend into the ether of the city, being nothing else but another denizen.

But then she'd remind herself of what she loved so much about the small town. The space. The lack of hurry. And of course, the animals.

Besides, it was in town that her mother and father were buried, and she didn't want to leave the only human family that she had. She was afraid she'd be far too lost if she left them.

But as she looked up at the disappointing sky, she realized that she wanted to see *real* stars. She bet if she got far enough outside of town, she could see what she was craving.

In fact, she was pretty sure she had seen a nice hill at the Miller Ranch. Surely, they wouldn't mind her hanging out on the property for a little bit as long as she didn't get up to any trouble?

Right?

She hoped so.

With some uncertainty, she grabbed one of her thick blankets and got into her car, heading toward the ranch. The drive was peaceful, with not a lot of cars on the road at midnight between Sunday and Monday, and she arrived without much fanfare.

She couldn't help but think that she probably shouldn't be at the Miller Ranch outside of work hours, but she couldn't imagine the welcoming and kind family being mad at her. If they even caught her.

Caught was the wrong word. That implied she was doing something wrong. More like... stumbled upon her.

But despite the dubious rule-breaking that she may or may not have been committing, she felt completely safe as she found the hill she had in mind and went ahead and laid her blanket out.

She stared up at the night sky and, just as she had suspected, there were way more stars visible out in the countryside. The sky took on a beautiful sort of visage, and Missy let her head drift up into them.

It was a bit funny. Often space seemed so far away that it was impossible to reach, but the truth was that if she somehow managed to drive her car upward, it would only take her an hour to reach it.

Just an hour and she could be out in the celestial mist, touching things that were impossible to touch, being away from Earth and all its troubles.

But in truth, she would miss all of her animals, and pancakes. Definitely pancakes. And the cool wind when summer was just shifting to autumn, then the warm gust of growth as winter faded to spring. As much as she mentally complained about Earth, and as much as she hated feeling the glares of those who were judging her, she liked to think that there were nicer things to love and appreciate.

Missy continued to stare up, feeling herself start to relax and drift away. It was always easy to forget everything when she was alone and quiet in the night. Easy to forget the path her Dad had fumbled down and how he had overshadowed her own journey in the eyes of everyone else. Easy to forget how their gazes went to her chest first, then her hips, and no matter what she wore, they would always find her too much because of what they found there.

A noise sounded behind her, shattering her relaxation. Scared of coyotes or other wild things that maybe had caught her scent, she jumped to her feet and whirled. But instead of a pack of creatures, there was a man standing there.

That didn't alleviate her fears at all, and she tensed as they stared at each other. She waited for the shoe to drop, for him to announce himself as friend or foe—or even react to her at all, but instead, he just stood there.

"Uh, hello?" Missy called uncertainly.

He still said nothing. For a moment she worried that he was trying to scare her with his silence, but no... that didn't seem to be accurate either.

Somehow, despite everything, she didn't feel in danger.

No. She felt...

Curious.

Carefully, she approached him, talking to him the whole time. She wasn't sure if what she was saying made sense, but it was just sort of general platitudes and offerings of comfort.

"Hey, are you okay, sir? Do you need help? My name is Melissa. Can I help you?"

But he didn't react at all, no threatening moves, no sudden lunges. He just stood there, staring at her.

No.

Staring *past* her. And the closer she got, the more she noticed that tears were streaming down his tortured looking face.

Oh.

She knew who this was.

It had been hard to make out his features in the low light of the hill, but now she knew without a doubt that this was another Miller brother. He was the talk of the town about a year ago when he came back from the army. He'd gone off to war right out of high school, and when he finally returned home, there was something a little... wrong with him.

Or at least, that was how most people looked at it. Missy had read enough to know about PTSD. After her mother had died and her father had suddenly turned into a completely different person, she'd done a whole heck of a lot of research.

Not that any of it had done any good. But perhaps it would now.

Missy stopped her footsteps. She knew how dangerous someone in a fugue could be, and she wasn't going to risk getting within his range. And judging by his incredibly *built* body, that was probably a considerable area.

"Hey there, I know you probably can't hear me, but I want you to know that you're all right. You're safe. You have nothing to worry about. I'm gonna be here, okay. Watching over you. How does that sound?"

He didn't respond, because of course, he couldn't, but Missy hoped that he could feel that he wasn't in whatever hellscape his mind was taking him off to.

5

Bart

*S*creaming.

Someone was screaming at him. Loud. So loud. And they wouldn't stop, thrumming through his ears and vibrating in his skull. He hated it. It made him feel sick. He wished whoever was screaming would stop.

There was a fire.

Where was it?

He didn't know. It just was.

He needed to find his troop. They were somewhere... weren't they? He tried to remember, but it felt like his head was stuffed with cotton.

Cotton that only made the screamer that much louder.

Bart reached around for his gun, but there was no gun. Was there anything? He didn't know. Did he? No, he didn't. There was just smoke. And the screamer.

And explosions.

Bart jumped, a shout issuing from his own mouth as multiple blasts sounded all around him, sending dirt flying and shrapnel everywhere.

No.

No.

This was supposed to be safe. They'd cleared the area. Weren't they supposed to be safe?

He cried out for any of his friends, his brothers in arms, but the only response was the screamer. He was lost. So lost. It felt as if he was never going to get out, constantly trapped in the smoke and the screaming and the nothing at all.

But then, up ahead, seemingly impossibly far away, was the tiniest spark of light.

A scope of an ally? A spotlight on top of a tank? It seemed... familiar. Hopeful. And it wasn't black or smoke or screaming or scattered bodies, so he stumbled toward it.

He reached it and was bathed for a moment in the warmth of it, gliding over his face and drowning out a little bit of the scream. But as he lifted his hand up to it, the light zoomed away, leading him further through the battle.

Was it a battle?

He couldn't tell.

Did it matter though?

He didn't think so.

He kept on walking and walking until finally, he stumbled into quiet, his ears ringing from the cacophony of battle he had just run from. Looking behind him, he saw the light slowly receding, winking out like a guardian angel that had done its duty.

How strange.

Then, just as suddenly as he was in that world, he was out of it, his eyes fluttering open as he awoke.

He laid there for a moment, head heavy, wondering what kind of strange nightmare he had been having when he noticed he wasn't in his room at all. After a bit of blinking and looking around, he realized that he was on the couch in the living room of the main house and that it was *way* too early in the morning.

He didn't remember being downstairs, and he was pretty sure that his mother would never allow him to crash on the couch when he had a perfectly good bed. But if he didn't want to get a lecture, he had better get up and get back to his room before she spotted him. It was a miracle she hadn't already.

Drawing the blanket around his shoulders as he sat up, he realized it wasn't his. It could be one of his brother's, he supposed, but it seemed to be machine-made whereas most of the blankets around the house were handmade by his mom or another family member.

More strangeness.

Shaking his head, Bart told himself that he probably didn't have a running inventory of every blanket in the house in his head and shuffled to the stairs.

It was only when his foot first touched the step that he realized his feet were not bare, which was his normal routine. Instead, strange, pink socks were on his feet, barely fitting over his ankles.

That was... odd.

Was it one of the many nieces running around? He'd lost track of them long ago. People just kept on having babies and reproducing like the world wasn't a terrifying place.

Which it was.

Part of the reason his dreams were so bad was because they were all based on what happened in the actual world.

The scary, cruel, unforgiving world that stole away people's lives in the blink of an eye and let the bad guys survive when they shouldn't.

Shaking his head, Bart trudged himself up to bed, hoping for at least another two hours of sleep.

That'd sure be nice. And maybe this time, he wouldn't dream.

6

———

Missy

*M*issy groaned as she stumbled into work, her back throbbing violently.

She had stayed up *way* too late following Bart around, making sure that he got back in his home safely.

It hadn't been easy, with him almost wandering into one of the ponds and nearly walking into fences. He was one of the rare people who was significantly larger than her, and she doubted that she could manhandle him.

But he did seem better with her there, talking to him quietly. He didn't respond, of course, but he did stop crying, and the look on his face seemed far less tortured. Even if he didn't respond verbally, she took that as a good sign and stayed with him until he was safe and on the porch.

Then he had stood there for a while, just staring at the front door. Missy hadn't been quite willing to go inside, but she did open the door for him and then put her own socks on his feet. His were muddy and covered in grass, but she figured that it was better for them to be dirty *inside* of socks rather than outside of them.

"Hey, friend, don't you want to go inside? Maybe have a little bit of a rest?" She remembered that she had been a bit uncertain about the whole thing, her eyes flicking between him and the open door.

The man's head tilted toward her, and for a moment it seemed like he actually saw her, but then he shivered, and she went into mom mode.

"Here, take this." She had draped her blanket over his broad shoulders and gave him the slightest pat on the back. She knew that being so close to him was dangerous, but she couldn't help it. He reminded her of some of her animals at their worst, scared and shivering and worried about each shadow that flitted across their path.

He'd finally gone in, and she'd hurried home to slip into bed somewhere around three a.m., only to wake up bright and early to get to work on time.

So now she was mucking out a stall and feeling exhausted in every fiber of her being. Even with her bath the previous day and all the relaxation over the weekend, her body was super mad at her for shorting herself on sleep.

But still, it was worth it. Or at least she thought so. She couldn't help but wonder how hard it had to be for the guy, and how bad his symptoms were if he was sleepwalking a whole year after getting back.

Was he getting treatment? Was his family even aware of how

serious his issues were? She didn't know, but she didn't think she should tattle on him yet. What if that got him in more trouble?

It was all sticky and confusing in her mind. Missy couldn't help but think back to her father, who was traumatized by watching her mother die in front of him. He'd never gotten treated, and it had definitely ruined his life and troubled hers. She didn't want this Miller brother to go through that, but she wasn't sure where the boundaries were considering she'd only been working there for about a week.

Besides, if she let on that she knew about him, she would have to explain *how* she knew about it, and that would open its own can of worms. What if his family reacted poorly? Maybe even institutionalized him? One could never know with rich folk. They were like an entirely different species to Missy, with her family having gone from middle class down to just below the poverty line as her father sunk deeper and deeper into his drinking.

"Hey, you okay there?" one of the other muckrakers asked, concern on his features. "You seem like you're coming down with somethin'."

"Just some insomnia," Missy said with a sigh, flashing him a weak grin. "Didn't get a whole lot of sleep last night."

"Ah, that's a real bummer." The man smiled and handed her the massive water canteen he had resting on a table beside him. "Why don't you take a break and go fill these up for a bit? Maybe some fresh air and sunlight will give ya a little extra pep to get through the day."

"Thanks," she said, wiping her brow and chucking her gloves off to grab his canteen and her own. She collected the other workers' near-empty water containers as well and headed toward the food cabin, where she knew there was plenty of ice that would fit into the narrow necks of all their drinks.

She really liked it at the Ranch, even if it was unusual to be surrounded by such nice people. And they really were nice. They watched out for each other; they laughed and joked. Everyone made her feel welcome. These were good people. She could probably trust them.

She splashed cold water on her face once she reached the sink in the food cabin, images flashing behind her closed eyes. It was the Miller brother who dominated most of them, and she took in all the details that her mind picked up. The sharp edge of his chin, his strong cheekbones, his thick hair. The scar.

And the tears.

Wet and torturous, streaming down that handsome, scared face. She didn't know him, but she hated the thought of *anyone* feeling like that. Especially anyone whose family was so nice to her and completely turning her life around by giving her a job that she didn't even have to apply for.

Maybe she should tell someone. Sure, she had worked with a vet and was really good with animals, *and* she liked to care for people—sometimes to a fault—but that didn't mean that she should go about making decisions for this man's health.

She sighed, finishing with her task and heading back to the barn. All this thinking just made her that much more tired.

Maybe she'd come to a decision *after* she got a full night's sleep.

7

Bart

rack!

The satisfying sound of wood splitting filled the air, and Bart allowed himself a small smile. He may not be very useful lately, but he could cut wood like nobody else's business.

Maybe it was the productivity that spoke to him. Maybe it was the manual labor. Maybe it was just exercising and doing things with his own two hands that helped his family.

Or maybe it was just—

Footsteps sounded behind him and alarm shot straight up his spine. Danger! Where were his weapons? What were his options? How could he let someone sneak up on him when he knew never to leave his back unguarded!

He whirled, heart thundering. All he could see was red,

terror telling him that he was weak. That he was stupid. That he was going to get himself killed because—

"Bart?"

The alarmed cry gave him pause, and a beat later he recognized that exact tone.

Ma.

Safety.

He was home.

The ax fell from his hands and his vision cleared, leaving him to look at the wonderful woman who now had tears in her eyes.

"Oh Ma..." he whispered, his heart squeezing in an entirely new way. He shouldn't be here. On the Ranch. He was just causing trouble. More trouble than he was worth. He was intrinsically broken, and they would all be better if they tossed him in a cell and threw away the key.

"I'm sorry for startling you," she continued, straightening her shoulders and moving on like everything was all right.

But it wasn't all right, couldn't she see that? He was supposed to be some big, strong *man*, and here he was, jumping at shadows and threatening the ones he loved. "Don't say sorry," he heard himself growl. "It's my fault. Ma, I think—"

"Let's not start with that again," she said, cutting him off before he could even get started. "I think though, perhaps your biweekly therapy might be better as a weekly appointment."

Therapy. Sure.

Yeah, it had helped him a lot when he first came home. Back then, both time and his memories were a slipshod of confusion and unease. He had been fine for a day or two, but then suddenly everything had crumbled all around him and the night terrors had started.

He'd been more dangerous back then, even attacking one of his brothers. They'd managed to restrain him and get him to a hospital that helped bring him out of his fugue and treat the injuries he had given himself in his rampage. But once he was cleared, they had taken him to a VA facility that was supposed to help with his issues.

He wished they would have just dumped him there and forgotten about him, but his Ma stayed the entire time, with his brothers and Pa visiting often. They apparently had their own classes at the VA, to learn about him. What to do when he was in a state, how to avoid certain triggers, and what to do with the ones that couldn't be avoided. It made Bart feel like some sort of *baby* that they had to attend special lectures to learn how to raise him.

It was infuriating, and at the same time it was comforting. Above all, it was embarrassing. It was a lot of things. Although Bart's memory was hazy, he remembered once how independent and intrepid he had been. An all-American boy.

Now he didn't even feel like a man.

Slowly, his mother raised her arms in a non-threatening gesture, then stepped forward. He knew what she was doing and allowed her to hug him.

"My boy, my sweet boy. It's okay. You don't have to carry this all on your shoulders."

But he wasn't carrying it. He was sagging under all the weight, feeling like he was drowning in things that weren't even really there.

He allowed himself to relax into the hug ever so slightly, letting himself feel the comfort that he didn't deserve. "Am I ever going to be better?" he heard himself rasp.

Sure, he'd heard about PTSD before, but it was like a

boogeyman. Something that couldn't touch him. He had thought he was too strong, too level headed and equipped for all of that. And now that he was standing in the center of it, trying to navigate toward whatever "normal" was, he couldn't help but wonder if he'd ever been strong at all.

"You will, Bartie, I promise." She pulled away gently but took his hands in hers. "Why don't we go for a walk? Soothe our nerves a little?"

He almost wanted to say no so that he could go barricade himself in his room and sulk for a while. But even through everything clouding his head, he always knew that he was a mama's boy, so he felt himself nod before his mind even caught up.

"Sure. That sounds nice."

She linked her arm in his and they got to walking. Bart didn't understand how she could be so calm with someone who had just raised an ax to her, but he probably would never understand his Ma. She was some sort of saintly paragon that was too good for his basic understanding of the world.

Or at least something like that.

They strolled along, arm in arm, and Bart let himself soak in the nostalgia. It was a bittersweet sort of torture to see all the places that used to bring him so much happiness. There were the hay bales that he and his brothers would pile up into irresponsibly high piles and monkey around on. There were the ponds that they would swim in when the summers were achingly hot. The birthing pens.

So many memories. Echoes of joy and ease that he never felt nowadays.

He tried to focus on the crunch of grass under his feet and

the sounds of the animals and the day to day work that went into running the farm. Those were safe noises. Things that had never been touched by the world that had gobbled him up and spat him out.

He heard a loud meow and looked to the sound. There, sitting on the fence post, was one of the cats who hung around. A friendlier one, the tabby looked to him expectantly.

Smiling slightly, he crossed to it and gave it a good scratch behind the ears.

"Hey there, guy. I normally don't see you here by the barn."

The cat purred, wrapping his tail around the man's wrist, before deciding he had enough petting. He jumped down gracefully and walked toward the barn. Bart watched him saunter off like the cat knew the meaning of life.

Bart was all set to return to his walk with his mother when he heard a sweet sort of cooing. Then someone walked out of one of the stalls in the barn, crouching down in the open center aisle to give the tabby even more affection.

Unlike with Bart, the cat lingered for more than five seconds, winding around the person's feet, rubbing his cheeks against their jeans.

"All right, I gotta go do some work. We'll talk later," the figure said, unfurling to reveal one tall and... solid woman.

She had long, blond hair in a ponytail, her tanned skin dappled with sweat. Dirt was covering a lot of her, but her bright red lips and ruddy cheeks were visible even from where he was.

The woman didn't seem to notice him, turning to pick up a pitchfork and haul another load of hay and manure. With her body turned to the side, he got to see the, uh, *impressive* conundrum of ideas she was.

Her arms were strong, the muscles rippling with each jab of her fork. Her shoulders were broad, and her movements spoke of someone who was confident and sure. She was like an Amazon, and she reminded him of several women soldiers he had known.

But then there was a softness to her. Her hips were wide, and there was a curviness to her body that gave her a feminine allure. And above her waist... well, it was easy to tell why she needed the multiple bra straps that were digging into her shoulders under her tank top.

She was basically the epitome of a bombshell, and Bart was sure that if he had a cousin who looked like *that*, he would have heard about it.

But then, just as he was staring, her eyes flicked over to him, as if she felt his gaze. Bart blushed a bit and raised a hand to wave, figuring that he could play it off as just a friendly family member saying hi to a new worker, but the moment their line of sight matched up, her eyes flew wide and she dropped her pitchfork.

She looked... *scared*?

That didn't make any sense.

Did she know who he was?

Word must have been getting around. Soon he was going to be the terror or the pity of the entire town; poor Bartie Miller, who got himself broken and scrambled in the head while fighting for his country, and all the riches in the world couldn't fix him.

"Are you all right?" his mother asked.

"I'm fine," he answered, tearing his eyes away. "Let's just keep walking, okay?"

"Of course. Whatever you need."

What did he need? Well, that was certainly a complicated question.

And maybe one day he would actually know the answer.

8

———

Missy

$\mathcal{M}$issy's heart thundered in her chest as she ducked back into the stall. She could feel her cheeks burning crimson.

Oh goodness.

Oh goodness gracious with a rotten cherry on top.

She hadn't *meant* to gawk at the man right out in the open, but he was about the last person she had expected to see.

And what a sight he was.

It was like an utterly bizarre change to see him in broad daylight. So strong, so assured. If she didn't know better, she would think that he was just another strapping Miller son. He was nothing like the hurt man that she had spent most of her night guiding to safety.

Was she exaggerating things in her own head? Projecting

things onto this man based on her own experience with her father? She supposed it was possible, but she didn't really have much to go on.

Maybe it would be best if she minded her own business and didn't start poking around in the Miller family's affairs.

Nodding to herself, Missy forced herself to get back to work, even if her back was practically weeping about it. But even as she cleaned the stall, her mind couldn't get away from that man. That tall, handsome man.

Sure, he was attractive, but that wasn't it.

Okay, so he was possibly one of the hottest men she had ever laid eyes on, and that certainly helped grab her attention, but that didn't feel like the reason why he was centered in her mind.

No... it was because for a moment when their eyes were locked, she swore that she saw someone as out of place and lost as she was.

Hah! That was silly. She really was only overtired and needed to get a good nap in. And the sooner she finished her work, the sooner she could do just that.

It didn't get any better after lunch. Her muscles were fatigued, and her thoughts were starting to get that particular sort of sleep-deprived syrupiness that made little sense and mostly whined a lot.

She didn't want to go back to the stalls, but she had to. She'd only been there a week, and she couldn't exactly shirk off her work. She needed to show her gratitude. That it was worth it that they had taken a risk on... well...

Someone like *her*.

So she found herself once again mucking out a stall, her frame screaming and her eyes constantly wanting to check her cracked phone for what time it was.

She forced herself to keep going, one toss after another until a sound broke through the drudgery.

It was so whisper-quiet that she almost didn't catch it at first. Stilling, she cocked her head, closed her eyes and listened.

There it was again. Tremulous, and almost impossible to hear. The tiniest little call for help, pleading for someone to answer the cry.

Missy followed the sound to the edge of the stall and dug through the old hay, searching and searching until she finally found the source of the plaintive cry.

It was a kitten. Tiny, dirty and bedraggled. Missy let out a coo and pulled her bandana from her neck, using it to pick up the kitten as she went to cradle it to her chest.

"Hey there, little one. Are you okay?"

It let out another mewl, barely audible. Oh, the poor thing. He'd been rejected, hadn't he? She looked him over. He was small, quite small, and he only had one eye, the other just a blank patch of fur. She turned him this way and that. He had fleas, and probably worms, but she could move all of his joints, and he was fully formed. No wounds either.

She could save him. Not that she knew he was a him, but to her, orange kitties always seemed like boys. She could check him later, assuming he survived.

Quickly, she took a mental inventory of everything she had at home. Antibiotics, deworming medicine, kitten formula. Yeah, she could definitely help him out.

"Hey, would you like it if I take you home?"

He let out another little warble, and Missy smiled. She really had a soft heart, didn't she?

"Hey guys," she said, wandering into the main aisle. A few of her fellow workers leaned out, looking at her curiously. "On a scale of one to ten, how bad would it be if I took off an hour and a half early to take care of this little one?"

"Are you sure you should do that? Usually, when a mamma rejects a kitten, it's for a good reason."

"I know," she said with a shrug. "But I've had some success with runts. I think he could be a good ol' cat if given a chance."

There was a collective shrug. "I mean sure. As long as you don't make it a habit. I can't imagine any of the bosses being mad. They're pretty understanding."

"Perfect," Missy said with a smile. "I'll see you guys tomorrow."

"Okay."

Missy hurried off, kitten still held to her bosom, and she piled into her truck. "Just hang in there, okay little guy?"

She drove off, praying that he'd be all right. Maybe it was silly to get so wound up over a kitten, but she had a weak spot for helpless things.

Luckily, he made it to her home, and she concentrated on getting everything ready for him. First some water, then formula, then washing, then the medicine. By the time she was rubbing his hindquarters with a damp cloth, trying to get him to relieve himself, it was already dark.

Geez, she was tired. She felt like she could just fall into bed and sleep forever.

But she couldn't. The kitten needed to be checked on every two to four hours. Oh boy, she was going to have a real rough week, but it would be worth it if the kitten pulled through.

Sighing, Missy set her alarm for two hours then slid into bed.

Missy awoke right on time with a groan, her alarm persistently howling. She rolled out of bed—an easy feat to do since her twin mattress sat on the floor. She crawled over to the little box that she had put the kitten in.

He was sleeping, but he mewled at her again when she picked him up, acknowledging that she was close. He wasn't old enough to have his eyes open, but she figured he was awake enough to feed.

Once more, she went through all of the steps of taking care of him until, finally, he was tended to and sleeping in her hands like a little butterball.

"We're off to a good start," she told the kitten before returning back to bed. "I'll drop you off at the vet's in the morning to get checked out and take care of those fleas."

But as she settled in, she couldn't get comfortable. She tossed and turned; then she tried reading for a bit. Nothing worked. Every minute she could feel precious time slipping away. She needed to go to *sleep*. Couldn't just one thing go right for once?

She tried to settle down, but eventually, she ended up on her back, staring up at the cracked ceiling of her studio apartment. There was something tugging at the back of her mind, whispering that there was something else that she wanted to do... needed to do.

What if the Miller brother was out in the open again? What if he got into trouble? It really wasn't any of her business, but...

Finally, after probably not that long at all, she groaned and got out of bed. A few moments later, she was throwing a flannel over herself and then driving back to the ranch. She had three hours before having to get back to the kitten.

She was being ridiculous about Bart. And she knew that. But the same compunction that made her want to take care of the kitten also made her want to take care of the strange soldier that she knew nothing about.

She arrived just as quickly as she had the first night and parked her truck. Making her way to the same hill with a new blanket in hand. She was being crazy. This was *dangerous*. And yet she kept on walking until she was on top of the grassy knoll, looking up at the velvet sky.

No one was there.

She let out a breath, not knowing if she was relieved or upset. She had wasted so much time, and not to mention sleep, only for no one to be around.

Sighing, Missy set out her blanket and went to sit on it, figuring she could at least stare up at the sky and feel some peace. But then she heard shuffling behind her.

There he was, walking through the grass, reaching for something she couldn't see.

It didn't even take her a breath to know that she had to help him.

Somehow.

9

Bart

Screaming.

Gunfire.

The never-ending clatter of tank treads moving. Crunching. Destroying.

It was loud. So loud. Why couldn't it just be quiet?

There were voices in the cacophony. They coiled around his ears until recognition sank in.

His friends. His brothers-in-arms. People that he knew and shared every day with. They needed him. He had to help them.

He stumbled around in the smoke and fog and terror, the ground shifting under him this way and that. He couldn't see anything, couldn't smell anything other than the acrid burn of war, but he had to find them.

The churning ground beneath him shifted into a burning fire, red-hot embers causing his feet to smolder. But he didn't care. Let the fire burn him. Turn him to ash and then maybe he would finally be clean. Reborn.

But until it did that, he needed to keep on searching.

No man left behind. Right? That was what he repeated to himself as he struggled through the inferno that was quickly swallowing everything.

The entire world was smoke and pain and fear. Fear of failure, fear he would never find them, fear that he was lost in a hellscape that he could never be freed from, but then it appeared again.

The light.

It was small, twinkling and weak in its incandescence, but it was there. The light beckoned him to follow without words and gestures, and yet he knew that was exactly what he had to do.

His body moved forward of its own, the terror and noise around him dulling ever so slightly. It led him through the flames, bit by bit until finally, he was in a calm sort of grayness again.

Bart took a breath for what felt like the first time in ages. The battle was gone. Had it ever been? He was—

The light flickered and then suddenly shifted, its form tapering and warping into a flashlight mounted on the barrel of a rifle that was about to fire.

No! He'd come too far and fought too hard to be taken away now. He dove for the gun, dove for his life, and his body clattered against the ground hard enough to rattle his entire frame.

He just wanted to go home! Why didn't they get that? Everyone around him was desperate and scared, and he felt like all of their feelings were drenched into every part of him until his soul was so full of their terror he might burst.

Something hit the side of his head, and the grayness started to spin away. He held on tighter to the rifle, the person who was *holding it struggling to wrest free. To kill him. To take everything away!*

He couldn't see who the other person was that was holding the gun, but he knew they were the enemy. That they wanted to kill him and take away everything he loved. He could see the tortured expression on Ma's face. See his brothers all standing in a line, trying not to cry. He had to stay alive, for them. He wouldn't let some demon in the night make them hurt so badly!

Another hit to his head then everything was swirling, and he was falling outside of himself.

Was this it? Was he going to die? Did he—

He landed back into himself, his rattling breath snapping him to reality as he straightened. His head felt like it was full of cotton, and everything around him seemed tilted as he tried to understand what was happening.

He was on the grass. The dampness of it seeped into his sleep pants, making his knees cold and clammy.

Outside the main house maybe?

Yes. He knew this hill. He and his brothers had sled down it during the really good snowfalls when they were younger. It was perfect for really long glides.

It was nighttime.

The stars were sparkling above. Different from the ones he had seen every night when he was overseas, but they were still beautiful.

It was a bit cold.

His feet were bare. Didn't he know to wear proper shoes outside the house? Certainly, his mother had drilled that much into him. Why was he outside anyway? He didn't remember needing or wanting to go anywhere tonight. Everything was worse while the sun was down.

Then he realized…someone's throat was in his grasp.

He looked down, his hands squeezing the tanned neck of the woman that he had seen in the barn that day. She was still beautiful, but something was wrong. Very wrong. Her face was red, with dirt streaked across one of her cheeks. Her hazel eyes looked up at him, bloodshot and with tears in the corners.

Fear. Terror. Everything he saw in her face was what he had felt. Odd, wasn't it—

Oh God, he was killing her!

She was gasping, one hand balled into a fist that reached up to slam into the side of his head again, and the other trying to pry his fingers from her delicate throat.

Bart threw himself back, his thoughts swirling and panic drenching the world in black. He curled to the ground, throwing his arms over his head and not daring to look at her body. No. No! *No!* This couldn't be happening! Why was she even on the ranch? Surely this was a dream. One of his messed up, walking night terrors that bit into his brain and didn't let him go until he was even more fractured than he was before.

But he could tell by all the sensations around him that this was indeed real. Her body, laying just a bit away from him, and the warmth in his hands from touching another human being.

He had finally done it. Snapped and killed someone like everyone said he would. He was too dangerous to be out. He should have been locked up when they first noticed how messed up he was.

There was no coming back from this. There was no forgiveness. He had done the unthinkable, and now finally, everyone would know exactly how far down into Hell he belonged.

10

———

Missy

ir rushed into Missy's lungs in a pained wheeze.

Ow.

Ow.

The black-speckled corners of her vision began to clear while her throat burned painfully, protesting at the trauma.

She had almost died there, hadn't she? She had felt her brain shutting down, her vision fading as her limbs had turned into lead weights. It had seemed impossible to get free, and yet she was.

She sat up slowly, her head throbbing as it tried to figure out exactly what had happened. She had been approaching the man carefully, calling his name as lightly as she could. But apparently, it hadn't been careful enough. Because when she kicked over a rock on accident, he had started like she had tried to shoot him, then tackled her to the ground.

It hadn't exactly felt pleasant, but she'd had worse in her life. Back before she filled out, she used to play football with the boys all the time. But then his hands had wrapped around her throat, and he started squeezing, and squeezing, and *squeezing* until the world had swirled away and halfway down a drain.

A cough forced itself out of her protesting esophagus, bringing her back to the situation. Right. She was on the Miller Ranch helping the son who had PTSD.

Her eyes shifted around, and she spotted the man in question only a bit away, doubled over on the ground, covering his face and shaking. Crap.

He didn't seem to be attacking her, or even in a state to think about attacking her, so she tried swallowing several times before speaking.

"I'm fine," she tried to speak, but instead it came out as a raspy sort of whisper. Barely audible. And certainly not audible over his wheezing.

Where did he come off wheezing, though, when she was one who had her throat squeezed shut just moments ago?

Her petty thought didn't help lighten the situation in her head like she hoped it would, but she pressed on.

"Hey, hey, I'm all right. You awake now? You stopped, so that means you're awake, right?" Her voice wavered between a barely there whisper and an annoying sort of squeak, and he didn't look up then either.

Darn.

She crawled a little closer. Then a little closer. Every moment drawing dangerously nearer made her heart beat that much harder. Her subconscious was going crazy, warning her that she was getting nearer and nearer to a man who had just tried to kill her. That she needed to tuck tail and run, run, run until she was far away from any sort of threat.

But she ignored it. She kept going bit by bit until she was close enough to reach out for him.

Missy had always liked to think that she was a brave person, but her hand was shaking as it tentatively stretched for him. She should go. Just being near him made her head dizzy and her mind bring up the myriad of uncomfortable sensations her body had. It felt like something was stuck in her throat—which was now very achy. Her head was pounding. Her blood was thrumming in her ears.

But still, she let her fingers just barely brush against the top of his hand as he shook.

"I'm fine," she whispered again, hoping he heard.

He snapped up like he was some sort of machine, and for a moment she was truly afraid that he was still caught in his fugue. But human recognition flashed within his eyes, and the next thing Missy knew, he was lunging for her.

Idiot! She was an idiot!

She didn't even have time to curse herself or react before he was pulling her into a tight hug, her front slammed into his hard chest.

Oh.

Oh wow.

That had been about the last thing that Missy had expected, and she froze there, awkwardly positioned on her knees with her upper half crushed to the form of the man as he breathed raggedly into the side of her neck.

For the tiniest of breaths, she remained rigid, expecting an assault. But as that passed, she realized this wasn't an effort to hold her down or take something from her. This was the desperate hold of someone who had thought that he had hurt her, someone who was more scared of the potential of what he could have done to her than anything else.

Carefully, her arms came up and encircled him too. Or encircled what they could. Geez, this Miller son was *big*. Obviously, she had always been able to tell that he was built before, but she guessed she had underestimated just how solid he was until she was pressed up against him.

Was it wrong to feel slightly distracted by the musculature pressing into her? The man was cut like a Greek statue, however, this didn't really feel like the time to focus on that. But with his strong arms pressing her to his firm body as if she was his last lifeline, it was difficult not to notice.

She blamed the town. Ever since she hit puberty and got a certain reputation from her body deciding to hit the gas pedal in the bust and hips category, she'd learned that the boys—and then men—that she interacted with normally wanted a singular thing. And that wasn't a relationship. Or some sort of fairy tale romance. No, it was something much more carnal than that.

As a result, she didn't really date, and she certainly hadn't been held like this in a very, very long time. Like she was the last bit of shelter in a storm, and the man in her arms was barely holding on.

The moments passed, and the man seemed to come to himself, his muscles stiffening even further—which she had *definitely* thought wasn't possible—as he probably realized that he was clinging to a woman he had just almost killed. Slowly, he sat back, and for the first time, Missy got an up-close view of what he looked like when he was fully aware.

Wow. He was handsome. But so handsome that it bordered

on pretty. He had a strong, masculine face with that classic Miller jaw and a defined, regal nose. His lips were entirely too kissable, and his green eyes were framed with lashes that were entirely unfair. In fact, the only thing that kept him from looking like some Hollywood hunk was the tortured expression on his face.

"I hurt you," he whispered, his voice as ragged as his breathing.

Missy nodded. Denying it would have been an insult to his intelligence, and she could tell from the way his eyes moved over her, taking inventory of her injuries, that he was not a stupid man.

"Yes. But I'm here, and I'm okay."

"I... I'm sorry," he said flatly, seeming to deflate with his words.

She couldn't blame him, what was he supposed to say? It wasn't like there was an etiquette class that taught the right phrase to use after narrowly avoiding violently asphyxiating someone.

"It's all right. You didn't mean to,"

That seemed to be the wrong thing to say, however, because his face grew stormy.

"No. It's not all right. I could have killed you." A thousand thoughts seemed to flash across his face.

Missy felt a bit guilty. If she didn't have her savior complex and hadn't rushed out here in the middle of the night, he'd probably be fine. A good majority of the situation was probably her fault.

But... what if he had accidentally hurt someone else? His mother, or a worker? What if he had fallen into a pond? Or mishandled a tool? She didn't think she was sorry, even if the situation hadn't exactly turned out for the best yet.

"But you didn't. Besides, maybe that's what I get for sneaking up on you."

His eyes widened at that, and she guessed he finally put together the part where she wasn't really supposed to be on their land.

"Why are you even here?"

She shrugged. "It's stupid."

He remained quiet, staring at her so unnervingly that she eventually continued. She figured it might as well be now or never. After being nearly strangled, it wasn't like she was going to be able to skulk around at work under the radar.

"Look, I know what's going on with you, and I have an inkling of why you might want to keep it away from your family. So, if you'd let me, I'd like to help."

11

Bart

Bart stared at the woman crouched in front of him, her knees damp from the wet grass. It felt like thousands of emotions were flooding through him, building on and mixing up in each other until they were a confusing mess.

There was adrenaline, of course. He always felt vaguely nauseous and panicky after coming out of one of his night terrors. And then there was confusion. How did he know if this was the real world? Sometimes the line between reality and the strange hellscape that was his brain was so blurry that it was hard to distinguish what was real and what was some strange illusion.

Thankfully, there was relief there too, seeping in at the peripherals of his mind, reminding him that he hadn't killed her. He hadn't crossed that line.

However, that relief was quickly tainted when he realized that he could see the red marks around her neck from where his hands had gripped her so forcefully, and that made his stomach heave several times.

One of the only ways he had been able to get through the days lately was the fact that he had never actually hurt anyone. Although he had come close so many times, like that incident with his Ma and the ax—he hadn't laid hands on someone since his first time in the hospital. Now that he was looking at this strange, bedraggled, and yet entirely beautiful woman who almost seemed to glow in the darkness of the night, he couldn't help but feel suffocated by his guilt.

The marks of his weakness were on her skin, red and angry and quickly bruising. Her skin was marred by the brokenness that lingered inside of him. He felt panic rising up in him again.

He was supposed to protect people. He was supposed to be a *man*. Men didn't hurt innocent women and—

His eyes looked over her for possibly the fifth time in as many seconds, drinking in as many details as he could. It was like she was an anchor, pulling him into the now and holding him there. Telling him that this was real, this was tangible. The screams and the dark couldn't reach him here, as bizarre as the situation was.

But what he hadn't noticed before were the bright fuzzy pink socks on her feet, the only bright pop of color in her casual clothes. They were the same style as the ones that had been on him when he had awoken that strange morning in the family room.

Bart looked back to her, to her bloodshot eyes, to the grass in her hair, and the tear tracks down her cheeks. He looked at her like she was some alien come to life because at that moment, it felt like she was. What kind of human snuck out in the middle of the night to help a man nearly twice her size fight against his nightmares? No one that he knew.

"Who *are* you?" he asked incredulously, taking her in.

It was then that his mind supplied that he had seen her before. On the farm. She had been the buxom woman who had been cleaning out the stalls. The one that had disappeared when they made eye contact. That had bothered him at the time, making him wonder if his illness had become such common knowledge that even a new worker was aware, but he was beginning to think that maybe it had been another reason entirely.

"My name is Missy Dominic. I'm one of the workers here on the Ranch."

"And your duties are staying after hours and wrangling a would-be murderer?" he asked cautiously.

He didn't know how to act in this situation. While things had been dangerous from time to time overseas, he almost always knew what to do. There were protocols and training. There were rules of engagement.

Here, in the real world with a strange woman staring at him, his handprints on her like he was some kind of beast, there was no rhyme or reason. He felt like he couldn't even tell which way was up.

"No," she blushed a bit, and if it had been any other situation, he might have thought the color looked pretty on her sun-kissed skin. "That kind of happened on accident."

"How does that happen on accident?"

Good, put the questions on her. Then he wouldn't have to think for a moment. He could just intake information.

Her cheeks colored further. "Well, back on that first night, I couldn't get any sleep. And I remembered that there was a hill here with such a great view of the sky and I thought I'd be able to do some amazing star-gazing."

He swallowed, looking up. Oh yeah, there were stars out. They were pretty, in a way that seemed entirely removed from his situation. Maybe she really was an alien.

"You do that often?"

"Not as often as I'd like. I, uh, have a thing for constellations and stuff. I like the cosmos, makes everything else feel...not so important."

"And that's a good thing?"

"Yeah, you know, when the world is feeling like it's closing in and every little thing seems like the absolute worst. I can look up at the stars and I know that, in comparison, everything that's bothering me really doesn't mean much of anything."

Huh. He had never thought of it that way.

"And so, you were out here, looking at the stars, when I stumbled across you?"

"Yeah, that's basically what happened."

"Did I—" he had to stop to take a breath. It felt like his mind was whirring, trying to keep up with everything. His worst fears were happening, and yet there was a woman in front of him telling him that it was all right. She was talking to him like he was a normal, everyday guy and not someone who'd just been squeezing the life out of her.

His stomach throbbed again. He had really been about to kill her, hadn't he? What would have happened if she hadn't managed to slug him a couple of times on the side of his head? How close had he come to hurting a civilian?

"Hey, you there?" she leaned in a little, her face coming closer to his. That pulled him out of the whirlwind in his head, and he blinked at her.

"I'm here," he answered quietly.

"All right. Good. And so you know, you didn't hurt me. You let me guide you back home and get you inside, and that was that. I was hoping that this would be similar." She grimaced. "Obviously it wasn't."

"Why?" he asked, still not understanding her. Although he may have been out of his mind, he knew what era they were living in. How dangerous it could be for a woman to be out alone with a strange man. "Why would you ever risk that?"

Another shrug. "It seemed like the right thing to do. You were in pain, and I was there to help. It wasn't like I was trying to psychoanalyze you or anything, which I'm not qualified to do. I was just getting you home."

"A lot of people wouldn't consider that a 'just' kind of thing."

He couldn't get her. He found his brain urgently trying to take in every detail of her. She was just as curvy as he had originally thought, but there was a strength to her too. A solidness to her arms and back and thighs, along with that alluring womanly shape that once upon a time had been quite a distraction to Bart.

He remembered before, when he almost seemed to be another person, how he loved to flirt with the best of them. He had a series of girlfriends, nothing serious like his older brother with his high school sweetheart, but fun little flings with plenty of kissing and holding, and maybe a little bit of feeling up where he wasn't supposed to as a godly young man. He was nothing like his youngest brother, Bryant, who was the definition of a cat on the town, but he wasn't a pious schoolboy either.

"I guess I'm not like most people."

Her voice brought his attention back to her visage. She had a heart-shaped face, with big eyes and full, cupid-like lips. She reminded him of a librarian, but perhaps in more of an adult-video sort of way than any actual, blue-haired keeper of books.

"Are you seeing a doctor?"

Her question reminded him that it took two to make a conversation, and he swallowed once more before answering.

"I am."

He still was trying to puzzle it all out. Why had she helped him? Why was she still here? Why was she acting so calm? Even though it had only been a few minutes since he had come to, he could already see the print around her neck darkening.

"Is what they're doing working for you?"

What a bizarre question to ask. Her eyes were getting more bloodshot, and he could still hear a roughness to her voice.

Obviously, therapy wasn't working for him.

Yet he found himself giving a more coherent answer. "We're trying different treatments," he said slowly. "I've gotten better in a lot of ways, with some symptoms fading, but the night terrors are obviously still a thing."

She nodded, her hazel eyes looking him over. But he still didn't see terror written across her features. Why wasn't she scared? She should be scared. Right?

"Do you want to talk about it?"

Talk about it? What? Who was this woman? Yeah, he knew her name and that she was a worker, but none of it was really computing. She looked young. Weren't there options for her in town? It was rare for a young woman not involved in the family or farm originally to come out to the ranch.

"No," he said simply, and she seemed to take that for that, not pressing him for answers.

"Okay then. Do you wanna get off the ground?"

Right. They were still both kneeling on the ground, the

damp soaking into their knees. The cool wind was beginning to chill him, and if *he* was cold, he was sure that she must be really cold.

"Sure. That sounds like a good idea."

He stood carefully, offering her a hand. She looked from it to him, and he realized that his hand might not have some good associations for her after what happened, but after a beat, she still gripped it and allowed him to haul her up.

Once they were both on their feet, he found himself staring at her again. He had no idea what to do now. They were off the ground, but what did that mean? Where did they go from here?

"Should we get you inside?" Missy asked, wiping the dirt from her hands off on her thighs.

"Yeah. That would probably be wise."

It felt like the world had been ripped out from under him, and he couldn't help but think that something was wrong. So very wrong. This woman wasn't reacting right, and it was making him feel confused.

"You coming?" she asked, already taking a couple of steps away.

Bart swallowed, trying to center himself. His therapist had told him that breathing slowly, counting with each inhale and exhale could help him, so he tried that.

They walked in silence, and it seemed that she was just as awkward as he was. The conversation was done, with not a single word spoken by the time they reached his front door. But there was nothing uncomfortable about the silence.

"Well, here you are," she said.

"Here I am," he responded slowly.

Her eyes went from him to the door, to the sky then the ground, before repeating the whole cycle over again.

He may not have known her that well, but he could tell that she wanted to say something. "What?"

If she took offense to his monosyllabic questions and answers, she didn't say. Instead, she blushed again and heaved a sigh. "Look. I, uh, I know that I'm not really supposed to be here after hours, and I might be breaking a rule and all, so I'd be real appreciative if you didn't tell anyone about it. Ya know, keep this between you and me?"

He couldn't help it; he stared at her as if she had grown another head. Because to him, it seemed exactly like that. He had almost just killed this woman, and definitely caused her bodily harm, but she was asking him to not tell anyone.

Was she crazy? He knew at least a hundred other people who would have used this opportunity to either sue the pants off his family or try to blackmail him. It was one of the reasons why he wanted them to put him away. Every moment he was out on his own, he was a risk to the ones he loved.

But this woman, with her blond hair, and womanly figure and too-knowing eyes didn't seem to care about that. Was this a trick? It had to be a trick, right?

"I won't tell anyone if you don't," Bart said.

She smiled gratefully at that. "Well, I mean you can tell, like, your therapist if you need. But I'd ask you to leave it at that."

His mouth was going dry the longer he stood there in the night, the anxiety churning within him. "I can do that."

"All right. Awesome. Good night then. If that's possible."

"Good night."

Somehow his body took him through the doorway, leading him to the large bay window in the sitting room. He watched her as she crossed to her vehicle, her shoulders back and her strides certain. She slipped into the truck like she hadn't almost just met her maker, and once more their gaze connected as she turned her head to look back at the house.

That moment sat for a while, his heart thundering in his chest before she threw her car into gear and headed out. He watched her until even her taillights weren't visible, before drifting to his room.

He didn't know what to think. Didn't know what to feel. When his mind came back to him enough to look around his surroundings, he saw that his clock said it was two in the morning. He knew that she started her day quite early with all the other muckrakers, so he wondered if she would call in sick.

Goodness knew she deserved a break. He resolved to try to keep an eye on things tomorrow and make sure she didn't get punished for taking a day off so soon into her hiring. He had only seen her around the ranch once, so she could only be a couple of weeks into her employment.

Settling into bed, he was surprised to find himself sagging into the mattress. He supposed it was just him coming off the adrenaline and shock, but still, he found the idea of sleep terrifying.

What if he did something again? What if he somehow hurt someone else?

He didn't know, and he certainly didn't get any answers from his ceiling. Instead, he drifted off, wondering about that strange woman and if she would ever show up to work again.

12

Bart

Usually, when Bart's eyes flicked open, it wasn't a great event. Although night terrors often plagued him, when he was able to just sleep, the break from consciousness was more than welcome.

Little snippets of death, they freed him from everything that weighed him down and depressed him so much in real life. During his dreamless sleep, he was no one. Not a soldier. Not a Miller son. Not even a human. That nothingness was a relief.

And yet, as the sun washed over his face from the window, he found himself fully rested and ready to work.

...that was strange.

He sat up, expecting the feeling to fly away with the bliss of his unconsciousness, but it persisted, urging him to his feet and into clothes for the day.

Huh, was this what it used to be like? Before everything changed and there was no solid ground anymore? He didn't know, but he wasn't complaining.

He headed down the stairs, intending to catch the family at breakfast for once. It wasn't much of a crowd considering Ben wasn't due in quite yet, and Benji wouldn't be back until the later afternoon, but it was still nice to see Ma and Pa and a couple of cousins.

"Oh, Bartie," she said, looking at him with warm eyes. "You're up early."

He was always up early. But he didn't tell her that. Usually, he laid in bed, utterly exhausted from the things that haunted his sleep until he eventually caught of few hours of dreamless z's. Just enough to be functional, never the full cup o' rest that he was feeling now.

"What's for breakfast?" he asked, quickly changing the topic from himself. He felt like he had to talk about himself too often, and after his bizarre night with the even more bizarre woman, it'd be nice not to have to think about himself for a while.

"Pancakes, sausage, over easy eggs, and toast. Eat up!"

He did, sitting down at the table with his family just in time for Ma to load up his plate with way too much food. And yet he worked through it, listening to everyone talk, letting himself enjoy the moment. When was the last time he had done something like this? It felt like ages.

Eventually, the meal ended, and his stomach settled from the unhealthy amount of carbs he had ingested.

"I think I'm gonna go help Bradley," he said, standing up and taking his plate to the kitchen. Normally Ben was the leader on the ranch, with Benji being second in command behind him.

But since both were out, it meant Bradley, the second-youngest was in charge.

Maybe one would think it'd go to Bart, the second oldest, but he was in no shape to be running their entire daily enterprise. However, that didn't mean he couldn't aid his brother for the day. If he was feeling like a normal human, he might as well do something productive.

"Oh, are you sure dear?"

There it was, that tenuous sound of pity and worry creeping in on the edge of her tone. He hated that tone. Almost as much as he hated the anxiety that curled in his middle when anything happened that took him by surprise.

"Yeah. I'm feeling good today."

"All right then. I'm sure Bradley will be happy to have you around. Goodness knows he prefers the behind-the-scenes more than the hands-on parts."

"Yeah, it'd be a shame to waste his math genius on a bunch of manual work."

Her smile was small. "You know, that's exactly what he says."

Bart managed a small laugh at that. "Yeah, it sounds like something he'd go on about."

While Bradley was very hard-working, the second-youngest of the Miller's sons had a near uncanny knack for mathematics. He could figure things out in his head in a snap and had a talent for anything involving budgeting or an organization chart. Maybe people would think that wasn't an important skill on a ranch, but it was invaluable to their family. In the years since he'd been helping Pa, and then eventually taking over, he'd trimmed a whole lot of fat and helped the entire family make better investments.

"I'll see you later," Bart said with a nod before heading out.

The sunlight felt good on his face, the morning breeze deceptive considering how warm it was going to get by the time mid-afternoon hit. He usually wasn't up and at 'em until eleven a.m. or later, so it was refreshing to be out so early.

Bart walked across to where he knew Bradley would be starting his morning. All of the workers generally knew what they had to do day-to-day, whether it was feeding the animals, or letting them out, or tending to the machinery. But, as with any operation involving multiple people and livestock, every morning involved a thorough walkthrough to check if anything surprising popped up. Any last-minute breaks or damages that needed to be tended to.

And that was where Bradley would be. He'd start on the edge of the ranch and work his way inward, checking in with the team managers of each group.

Bart was so focused on getting to his brother before he hit the more complicated groups, that he didn't notice exactly where his path was taking him. It was only when he heard some grunts and several begging meows that he realized he was passing the barn.

His eyes flicked to the open doors despite his best efforts to stop himself, and sure enough, he saw Missy there, taking a long drink from her canteen as she leaned against her pitchfork.

Crap.

Even from where he was standing, he could see the flush to her face and the increased rise and fall of her chest with her strained breathing, but his eyes quickly went to the dark blue and white bandana around her throat.

Guilt rose up in him again, making bile rise in the back of his throat. Before he could skulk off, she caught his gaze and gave him a bit of a shy wave.

She wasn't angry? Last night he figured that she might have been in a bit of shock and that's why her response had been so strange. But it was the next day, and she was still acting as if nothing was amiss.

Dear Lord on High, he had almost *killed* her. She should be way more upset.

"Oh hey, Bart."

Bart nearly jumped out of his reverie and turned to see Bradley looking at him curiously. "What are you doing here?"

They were nowhere near the edge of the ranch, and there was equally little chance that he had gotten that far in his walk around. So why was he there?

"Oh, I decided to shake things up a bit. Start from the center and work my way out. What're *you* doing here. You usually don't leave the house until around noon."

Bart shrugged. "Just had a good night's sleep."

"Fair enough. You know her?"

He could feel his back tense and fought hard to keep it from his face. "Know who?"

"That pretty blond who was waving at you."

He hated lying to family more than he already had to, but he didn't see a way out. He didn't want her to get in trouble for being on their property when technically she shouldn't have been, and he didn't want his family to know that he was the one that had bruised her neck. They already walked a little bit on eggshells around him, and he didn't need any more of that.

"She's one of our workers, but I figure it would be rude not to wave back to a lady."

"Uh-huh."

To his credit, although Bradley was a whiz with numbers, he didn't always seem the best at reading people. Even his own brothers. Still, Bart was grateful when he appeared to have bought it.

"But why is she waving at *you*."

Or maybe he didn't buy it.

Bart shrugged, remembering the time they shared last night. "We're the boss' sons. She probably just wants to be polite."

"Fair enough. Anyway, I should get back to my walkaround."

"Yeah," Bart said halfheartedly before remembering the whole reason why he was even outside. "Do you want some company? Figured I could come with ya, help with some things."

"Really? Yeah, that'd be great. You know, I've done this before, but I still can't help but always feel like I'm going to ruin something."

Hah, was Bart certainly familiar with that feeling. "Don't worry, you won't ruin anything. That's my job."

Bradley laughed, and for a moment Bart felt like it was old times again, back when he always had a quip on the tip of his tongue and could make any of his brothers dissolve into a barrel of mirth.

He wasn't that guy anymore, but maybe—every once in a while—he could pretend to be.

"COME ON, Lola, hold still, would ya?"

Bart struggled to hold the calf's head still without hurting her. But Lola was at that stage between bandy-legged youngling and being a real tank, so she had quite a bit of power to her.

"She's fiery, isn't she," one of the workers said.

Rob, was it? Bob? *Steve*? Bart didn't know. It was hard enough that he and his brothers all had names starting with the letter B.

Keeping track of all their cousins, step-cousins, and third cousin's fiancé was nearly an impossible task.

"Yeah," Bart grunted before he was finally able to slip the nose-tag into place on the young cow's nostril. It wasn't a painful thing, but it certainly wasn't going to be comfortable for a while. "But it'll be better for everyone if she's tagged. You guys got yours?"

"Almost," another grunted.

Chris maybe? Yeah, he looked like a Chris.

"We still have four more to do. You wanna grab another?"

"Sure."

Bart headed over to the table where they had several more tags ready and waiting.

While incredibly annoying to put on, the little bits of thick plastic were vital to the health and happiness of their cows.

Seeing as they didn't separate calves from mothers, sometimes there was an issue where the young calves would aggressively chew at and hurt their mother's udders and each other's ears. It wasn't purposeful, but it was well-known that young cows sometimes never got over the mouthiness of their nursing stage and would try to suck milk out of anything they could get into their mouths, even when their teeth were grown in. Unfortunately, if not stopped, this habit could result in momma cows losing their udders or other calves losing their ears.

Strangely enough, all it took was a bit of a nose tag, a small bit of plastic that hung down from their nostrils, to stop that entire habit. It was a cruelty-free way of stopping a terrible phenomenon, and he knew that several of the young girls on the farm loved to come and decorate the tags with non-toxic paints to distinguish the calves from each other.

He probably would have been a lot more nervous being so

close to the barn, but he could only see the side of the building from the field they were in, so he didn't really have to worry about running into Missy.

But he also kind of wanted to run into Missy.

It was the dumbest conundrum going on in his head. Part of him wanted to stay away from the woman and her eyes that saw right through him and bore the marks of his weakness. But another part of him wanted to look at her again, taking in every feature and detail until she was burned into even the deepest corners of his mind.

He was being stupid. He really was.

And it wasn't like he had agreed to help with the nose-tagging process because it gave him the chance to be close enough to her to maybe see her—but far enough so he wouldn't have to interact with her. No, that certainly hadn't been his intention at all.

It was just that during his walk around with Bradley, this handful of workers seemed to need the most help and Bradley had never tagged a calf in his life. Yeah, that was it exactly. Calves were bouncy little tornadoes of grass-eating destruction, and the five workers could certainly use another pair of hands.

"Hey, it's almost time for lunch, right?" a worker asked, brushing off his hands.

"Actually, I think we're right on the money," the one Bart decided was Steve said, wiping his forehead. "You joining us?"

It took Bart a moment to realize that the man was talking to him, but he couldn't gather his attention enough to answer him. The muckrakers were all filing out of the barn toward the worker house, and his eyes were trying to pick Missy's form out of the mass.

She came out last, several barn cats winding around her feet while she bent down to pet each of them. He could practically hear her cooing at them from where he was and had the faint urge to find out what her nails would feel like gently scratching against his own scalp.

Steve interrupted his thoughts. "Hey, Miller's son, what are you—*Ahh*. I got ya. Eyeing the new girl, huh?"

Something in his tone pulled Bart from his wandering thoughts, a shiver of cold sliding down the back of his neck. Turning, he looked to the man, raising his eyebrow with an unspoken question.

But then he remembered words were a vital part of communication and cleared his throat. "What do you—" he started to say, but before he could get the rest of the words out, Steve came up alongside them.

"Do you see that kerchief around her neck?" he questioned, his tone also taking a turn that Bart knew he definitely did not like. "One of the barn workers told me when we were both getting water that she's got a real rough ring around her neck. Like a pair of man's hands. Her eyes are all bloodshot too. Looks like someone had a real go at her."

Bart went completely cold. They knew. Everyone knew. Word would get around, and then she would confess. And he would have to admit that she was telling the truth, even if it meant that he was going to lose everything that he'd worked so hard to build. The part of him that had been longing to be locked away, for a simpler life, for an existence away from the worry and anxiety...was pleased about the thought. But the part of him that wanted to be better, to get well, to be who he was before everything ruined him, didn't like the thought at all.

He took a breath, ready to tell the young men that they were assuming the worst about a situation, but then the conversation went in a completely different direction.

"Oh," another worker mused, coming over to join the growing lineup of young, twenty-something men and Bart. "She's one of *those* kinds of girls. Guess I shouldn't be surprised, given what I heard about her and that coke-bottle body of hers."

"Yeah," another commented. "She looks like the type to chew a man up and spit him out. Wonder if that's why she worked her way here. Already tore up most of the town and hungry for her next meal."

Bart could hear the leer in his voice. The cold in him snapped, and he felt himself quickly growing warmer and warmer with every word out of the young men's mouths.

"I know I wouldn't mind getting to know what she's all about," one of the workers said.

The heat grew, burning higher, making it hard to breathe. But Bart held himself still, fighting against the fury his body was urging him to slip into. He could feel himself teetering on the precipice like he hadn't since his first attack on his family all those months ago. He didn't want to lose himself to the beast, but clamping down on that took all of his energy, leaving him unable to speak up in the mystery woman's honor.

"Well you better have some rope on you, looks like she's into that," Chris said.

Steve shook his head. "Nah, the guy said those are totally hand marks. She's probably one of those internet girls with Daddy issues who just wants some big, strong man to throttle her."

"Hey, you wouldn't have to ask me twice." Chris laughed.

Why was he laughing? None of this was funny. It was cruel,

and it made Bart want to lash out. How *dare* they. They didn't even know this woman! How she put herself at risk for others in a way that made no sense.

Chris spoke up again. "Marking up a woman like that, well every man ought to at least once in his life."

Another joined in. "And with her type, you don't even stick around in the morning. Not unless you want seconds, of course. Women like that are so eager to please—"

"*Stop*," Bart hissed, his own words surprising even him. He stood to the side, his temper quickly ramping up to a point where he wouldn't be able to control it. Sure, he had noticed Missy's generous curves and her angelic face completed with sinful lips. And maybe he'd had some attraction spring up in him that he hadn't felt since before he left for boot camp. But *never* would he talk about her the way these young men were. Like she was a piece of meat. Some well-worn couch that they were all daydreaming about taking into their homes then discarding when they were done.

He didn't like the way they were talking about Missy, and he didn't like the assumptions they were making. This wasn't the type of talk that most workers were supposed to say on the farm. Why were these men being so crass? They reminded him far too much of his army buddies but not in a good way. When the desperation and loneliness got so intense that men said things they normally wouldn't in polite company.

"Aw, come off it boss," Chris said with a laugh. "We're just having fun. Besides, practically everyone under thirty knows who that girl is. She's got a bit of a reputation."

"That *woman* is a *lady*, and you will refer to her as such," Bart growled, the world going white-hot at the edges.

But Chris just snorted. "Yeah right. She's the daughter of the town drunk, and she's practically been running around on her own since tenth grade. Body like that, naturally she's had plenty of time to get into things." He smirked like he thought he was the funniest man on the Earth and Bart felt his fingers curl into fists.

Bart was storming forward, arm lifting from his side before the worker even finished his sentence. But before he could land the blow that would shut the man's disgusting mouth, a sharp call broke through the stormy haze within him.

"Bart!"

Bradley's shout was enough to bring him back to reality, and the second oldest of the Miller boys slowed to a stop, blinking. The workers seemed to understand that something had shifted and scuttled off, much quieter than they had been just minutes before.

Oh.

This wasn't good.

Bart stood there, chest heaving. His body was pumping adrenaline from being in full-on attack mode. He had wanted to *hurt* those men. To make them shut up and regret ever saying those terrible, judging words.

"Hey, you all right?"

Bart shook his head. He felt like it was all he could do. The world was crumbling around the edges, and he could feel his feet being pulled down into the churning, malevolent maw that was always within him.

"Do you need to get away for a bit?"

He nodded. But even that action felt like too much. Like he was clawing to get out of his own skin. He could feel the smoke and the screams and the darkness rolling back in, starting to blot out the light of day.

"All right. Take the rest of the day off. Do you need me to walk you back to the house?"

No. The house wouldn't help him right now. Nothing could. He was stuck in a broken, crumbling mind that kept putting danger where there was none. A mind that refused to let him have peace. It wanted to punish him for all that he had done, and all he hadn't done.

Unless...

Perhaps there was something that could help him. But it was selfish. If he was a good man, he would tuck tail and walk himself into the nearest pond to never surface again.

But if there was one thing that he had learned, it was that he wasn't a good man.

Turning on his heel, he marched past his younger brother and his concerned expression. Over the grass. Across the path. Until finally he was in front of the barn where Missy was still playing with the cats, cooing and murmuring sweet praises that made some of the darkness around him ease back.

She was covered in dirt and hay and sweat, but with the sunlight hitting her, making her tanned skin glisten as she poured affection over the creatures at her feet, Bart couldn't help but think that she was the most beautiful woman he had ever seen.

"Hey," he said, his voice sounding monstrous even to him.

She stood up sharply, her eyes going wide. But instead of horror or alarm, her face split into a friendly smile. "What's up?"

She was too nice. She had to be faking, right? Some animal instinct in her telling her that he was dangerous and the only way to be safe was to play along.

But despite that dark whisper inside of him, he found his mouth opening. "Is that offer for help still on the table?"

She nodded, her face growing even more surprised. "Yeah, of course. What do you need?"

"Are you free for a talk?"

13

———————

Missy

*M*issy walked beside Bart as they headed to the same grassy knoll where they had met. Perhaps it was a bit morbid to go back to that scene, the one where she had been flat on her back with his strong hands squeezing the life out of her, but it seemed to make a weird kind of sense. It was a chunk of the world that was only theirs. No one else knew of it or what happened there.

As they drew closer, her heart only began to pound louder, supplying her mind with snippets of what had happened before. Little flashes of memory and sensation, she shoved them down within her.

But even as she tried to bury them, they still flicked across her mind. How cold the dew on the ground had felt as it soaked through her shirt. Just how heavy the man was atop her, his thick, muscled thighs pinning her own legs to the ground as she tried to kick. The stars above, growing dimmer with every second.

And finally, the fear.

Sure, there was her own, but the man above her looked absolutely petrified, tears running out of his eyes as if *she* was the one trying to kill *him*. Which was exactly what she assumed was going on in his mind. So, once she was alive and very much not strangled, she resolved not to hold the action against him.

And for the most part, it was pretty easy. He was like one of her wounded animal patients who had clawed or bitten her when they were scared. If she resented every one of them, she would never get around to helping them.

Still... she was a bit surprised that this particular case had actually asked for help. She was sure that after he hadn't returned her wave from earlier, he wanted to pretend that she didn't exist. She couldn't blame him, but the idea certainly... stung a bit.

They reached the top of the knoll and he sat down, leaning his back against one of the few trees there. Missy plopped onto her butt across from him and internally told her heart to calm down before it gave her an apoplexy.

But instead of talking, the man sat there, looking past her like she was another specter from his illness. She tried to be patient. Tried to school her features into an expression someone mature and knowledgeable would wear. But eventually, that wore thin.

"So," she asked hesitantly, not wanting to bother the man but the curiosity eating her up inside.

"So?" he repeated noncommittedly.

"You said you wanted to talk?"

"I did."

She waited again and still nothing. Oh boy. This was going to be one of *those* kinds of conversations, wasn't it? One where she had to dig and pry and wrest a response out of him. Great.

Well, she had said that she wanted to help, and if this was how he needed help, then she guessed that was what she had to do.

"How are you?" Might as well start simple.

"Not good."

All right, that was a start. "Is there a reason for that?"

He nodded. And that was it. Okay, so it seemed that it was still her turn to speak.

"Did whatever made you feel not good trigger an episode?"

Another nod.

"Okay, so you needed to get away. Do you want me to distract you?"

One last nod and Missy smiled. Distraction was something that she could do. "All right then, that's in my skill set. Mama used to say that I'd talk a Chatty Cathy into the ground, so prepare thyself."

Honestly, she was pleased that he had come to her at all. Her father never seemed to understand what things triggered him going into depressive, alcoholic spirals, no matter how much she and court-mandated therapists worked with him. Whatever had happened with Bart, he had removed himself from the stimuli and sought out something to drown the alarms that were no doubt ringing throughout his body. That showed an incredible amount of strength—and a desire to get better.

But at the same time, being that strong all day had to be so utterly exhausting. Not just in a physical sense, but in a mental sense too. Always being on guard, ready for a million and one things that could set him off at any time. It was no secret that the world was a cruel place, with plenty of people intent on ruining other people's day just for the hell of it.

No wonder he was having night terrors where he wandered alone, looking for a relief that he couldn't find.

"So, what would you say your favorite color is?"

He looked at her curiously, but the randomness of her question seemed to shock some of the darkness out of his gaze. "My what?"

"Your favorite color."

"I... I guess I never thought about it."

"Oh nonsense," Missy said, feeling herself picking up speed as she gained confidence. "Everyone has a favorite color. Or I guess I should say color set—because I don't really have a *single* favorite color. It's like a range of hues."

"Uh-huh," he sounded suspicious, but suspicious was better than crying or shaking with rage, so she would take it.

"Mine is basically the purple-blue spectrum. I love it all. Somedays I'm more into blue, other days I'm more into purple, but they're just so *pretty*." She closed her eyes, picturing hundreds of beautiful shades and pigments. "I think the universe was built around how beautiful the purple-blue spectrum is. You know, with the ocean in all its various intensities. Water in general. *Space*! I mean, we all know that the best science pictures are always about those pretty space clouds and miasma.

"I also figure that's why people love blue eyes so much. How sparkly they are and all that jazz. I'm sure there are other reasons for it, but I like to think that—"

"You really do have a knack for this, don't you?" Bart interrupted, looking at her with a wry smile on his face.

"So I've been told." She returned his grin. "Ready to tell me your favorite color now?"

"I guess I've always liked green."

"Green?" she repeated, a bit surprised. Normally she had to wheedle a bit more to get guys to admit they dared like any color that wasn't black or camo.

"Yeah. It's the color of living things. Of spring and growth. Everything important seems to be green or blue, and I'm more tied to the Earth than the water."

"Fair enough," she said, feeling something strange in her chest.

Green, huh? The color of life? That was surprisingly poetic. She wondered who this guy was before he had gotten so sick from the trauma. He seemed like someone she would have gotten along with.

"So, is this what you do?" he asked, his eyes hardening again.

"What do you mean?"

"Pick up dangerous people and talk to them about what colors are the best?"

"Well, I do spend a lot of times with strays, now that you mention it."

That smirk grew ever so slightly bigger. "Is that what I am? A stray?"

"I dunno, are you?" She batted her eyes at him, enjoying the banter. She couldn't remember the last time that she was able to just joke around with someone. Usually, any sort of friendly words out of her mouth to a man between seventeen and ninety always seemed to be perceived as some sort of flirtation.

"I think I've got way too nice of a house and family to ever be considered a stray."

"That's true. Your guys' place is pretty darn nice."

"That's one way of putting it."

"But do you feel like you belong there?"

"What?" he answered too quickly, and she realized how insensitive her questions might sound. She hurried to explain, to prove that she had been joking.

"That's the difference between a cat and a stray right? Cats who feel like they belong will never not have a home, while ones who don't feel welcome will always be strays."

Bart rubbed his chin. "I'd say that's accurate, but what about dogs?"

Missy laughed at that. "Dogs are never strays as long as there's a human around to love them. They're a little more trusting than cats."

"So am I the cat and are you the dog in this situation?"

"I dunno," Missy said with a laugh. "I don't think I've ever taken kindly to being called a dog."

His eyes shot open a little wider. "I didn't mean—"

"I know, I know," she said softly. "But I couldn't resist. I don't think I'm much of a dog, however. I'm not exactly trusting."

"But you trust me."

Huh, this conversation was not going the way that she thought it would. "Who said I trust you?"

"Well, you're here right now, aren't you?"

"I am. But just because I want to help you, and I believe you wouldn't hurt me on purpose, doesn't mean I fully and blindly trust you."

"I already hurt you," he said, gesturing to her neck.

She rolled her eyes. Was he going to bring that up all the time? Because she was already over it. "Wouldn't *purposefully* hurt me."

"You have no way of knowing that."

"I guess I'll just have to trust my instincts then," she countered, feeling a bit daring.

"I used to do that."

"Do what?"

She watched as a myriad of expressions crossed his face. "Trust my gut. Believe in myself."

"And you don't anymore?" She had certainly tried her hardest to keep the conversation away from anything too serious, but it seemed like that was what he wanted to talk about. And if Bart felt comfortable enough to wanna talk about who he might have been before the world crashed down on his head, then she was ready to listen.

"I can't even trust that what I'm seeing is real."

Carefully, Missy reached forward, letting her fingers just barely trace along his arm. "*I'm* real."

"Yeah, I've figured at least that much out." He looked up, squinting at the sun. Missy took in the tan pillar of his neck as it craned upward, the sun lighting up his striking features. He really would have been quite the handsome man if it weren't for the tortured expression on his face.

Oh, who was she kidding? Even looking absolutely miserable, he was certainly a nice bit of eye candy. It also helped that when he looked at her, he seemed to see an actual human and not just a rack that could talk occasionally.

"I used to think that I knew everything, that I was one hundred percent certain of how my life was gonna go."

"Huh, that sounds kinda cocky to me," she joked.

"That's probably because I *was* cocky. I had a sort of confidence in myself that seemed unshakable at the time. I could make anything into a joke, and I was good at pretty much everything I tried.

"And then I went into the Army, hoping to serve my country, and I was good at that too."

She watched his eyes close and different shadows crossed his expressions. Ones less caused by sun and more by what was going on in that head of his.

Missy found herself wanting to reach out again, to slide her fingers over his face and soothe away the worried lines that were creased into his features. But they weren't nearly close enough for that. She was just a woman who he happened to run into in the dead of the night when he was in a compromising position. Nothing more.

"Maybe I was too good at it, and that's why I'm being punished now."

Missy's heart ached. How many times had she heard her father saying that her mother's death was punishment? Too many. And she found that she didn't like the sentiment coming out of this man's mouth either.

"You're not being punished. Your brain is just reacting to trauma. Everyone handles such things differently, and a whole lot of veterans are going through the same things you are."

He shrugged. "It feels like punishment."

"Yeah, I understand that. But I need you to know that it's not."

He turned his face away from the sun, looking at her once more with half-lidded eyes. With his pupils so dilated, the green of his gaze was particularly intense. "My mind might know that, in a way. But my heart doesn't believe it."

"Fair enough."

The moment quickly grew too heavy, weighing at the air and making it thick and suffocating.

"I think lunch is almost over," she said finally, wiping her hands on her work overalls and going to stand.

But quick as a whip, Bart's hand shot out, barely grabbing onto one of the loops along her pants. "Don't go. Please. I don't want to be alone right now."

So many things happened in her head at once. First, her heart broke. This guy sitting down on the ground in front of her had a massive family, plenty of workers coming in and out of his house, at least four other brothers that she knew of, but he still felt alone. What kind of life was that?

Secondly, she felt worry. What if she said something that screwed this guy up worse? Part of her responsibility as a vet tech was to only try to take care of animals that were within her purview. If she didn't know how to treat one, she took it to a vet or a clinic where it could receive the proper care. She wasn't a doctor or a counselor. Being overconfident would only hurt whoever she was trying to help.

Thirdly, she felt such a deep ache in herself at seeing such a man so broken. She wanted to save him, to build him up. To soothe over all of his wounds until he was happy and healthy. One of her father's therapists had warned her of this. That her urge to help and heal people could lead to her own undoing. She could easily see that happening here but could only faintly hear the voice in the back of her head telling her to slow her roll.

"All right," she said after a moment of breathing. "I'll stay. But I'm definitely going to need you to tell your brother."

"Of course," he patted his pockets until he finally pulled out what looked like a very basic smartphone. His fingers slowly worked across the screen until he tucked it back into his pocket.

"I texted him. Told him you were working on a project."

"Thank you. I'd prefer to stay out of trouble if I can."

He smiled again, but it was a bit more bitter than she liked. "Yeah, you've done a pretty terrible job at that so far."

"True, but it introduced me to you, didn't it?"

"I'm not so sure that's a good thing."

Ow.

Silence fell between them again and the moment grew even heavier. Clearing her throat, Missy figured it was distraction time again.

"So what's your favorite movie?"

He blinked at her again, clearly having not caught onto the pattern yet. But it wasn't frustrating. It was... endearing. In a way. Not that she needed to be endeared to a mega-rich heir who probably wouldn't have given her the time of day if a series of extenuating circumstances hadn't suddenly thrust them together.

Bart tilted his head, thinking. "I'm not sure I have one of those either."

"I know what you mean. I don't have *one* favorite movie, but I've probably got one per genre. So basically..."

THEY TALKED. About anything and everything. From movies to food to which animals looked like they shouldn't be real and what mythical creatures totally should be real. Interspersed between the nonsense were far more serious topics. Like how it was when Bart first shipped out. How many men he lost in his unit. How long he'd been struggling since he came home. His coping mechanisms.

Missy could tell that he was still leaving plenty out, but she understood. The fact that he was telling her anything at all had to be pretty darn significant. She was sitting across from a man who obviously didn't trust strangers, and yet he was trusting her.

The sun tracked across the sky unnoticed, and she couldn't remember the last time she had felt so at ease with another human. Bart didn't want anything beyond her words, he never judged, no matter how bizarre her non-sequiturs were. Missy tried not to let herself get ahead of things, but it felt like he was a friend.

Wow. A friend. When was the last time she had one of those?

Probably senior year of high school, if she recalled correctly. Her best friend in the world, and possibly the only person she trusted with all the dirty secrets of her family life, believed a rumor that Missy had slept with her boyfriend.

Missy didn't know how that had started, considering she loathed the guy and did her best to avoid him, but that was all it had taken for Sarah to throw away all their years of friendship. Although that was five years ago, Missy hadn't trusted anyone since.

Besides, they lived in a small town, so word got around about her so-called proclivities quickly. Most people wanted nothing to do with her, scared she would seduce their partners or otherwise corrupt their perfect life.

Her phone alarm went off, and she pulled it from her pocket. "Holy cow. The work day is over. I can't believe it."

Bart blinked at her again. She'd come to like that surprised expression on his face, like he was trying to add up factoids that didn't make sense to him.

"Wait, really?"

She nodded and showed him her phone. "Yeah, check it."

He rubbed his jaw, and reality seemed to weigh back down on his shoulders. She hated that. For a few hours, she felt like she had given him an escape that was well-deserved. But now she was going to go home to her pets, and he was going to go home to his family who didn't quite understand, and all of that work would probably come undone.

"Would you like to come to dinner?"

Now it was Missy's turn to blink owlishly at him for several moments. "I'm sorry, what?"

"Would you like to join my family for dinner? Ma is always looking to feed guests."

She continued staring, her body seeming to forget how to blink. Sure, they'd had some great conversation, but that wasn't the same as her meeting his family. What about the bruise on her neck? What about him hiding what he had accidentally done to her?

She swallowed, her mouth dry, but the words wouldn't come. His piercing eyes looked through her, clearly trying not to have hope within them.

Who was this guy, and why did she feel like he was only going to get her in trouble?

14

Bart

Stupid! Stupid! Stupid!

Bart tore himself to shreds as Missy stared at him, her hazel eyes wide with alarm and uncertainty.

What kind of idiot was he? Inviting the woman who he nearly killed to dinner with his whole family? Hadn't she already expressed wanting to stay under the radar, and yet there he was, asking more of her.

He hadn't thought the question through. Just like everything lately, he was too impulsive. Too emotional. But even though he knew that, too much of him didn't want her to leave his presence just yet.

Talking with her over the hours had been like someone taking him outside of himself and putting him into a body that works. No random shots of adrenaline. No sudden, over-whelming feelings that someone was trying to kill him. No confusion. No fugue. Just simple conversation with a woman who was as unpredictable as she was comforting.

It didn't hurt that she literally looked like an angel as she lounged across from him, shifting this way and that in the dappled shade of the tree. And when a ray of light did catch her, she was dazzling. Her blond hair shone gold while the illumination drew attention to all of her features that were entirely too alluring. He could list them all off without hesitation, the sights burned into his mind like a brand.

There was the defiant arch of her brow whenever she was being snarky or sarcastic, and goodness, the girl had plenty of sass to call upon. There was the smooth scoop of her cupid's bow above her plush, always-moving lips. Even the way it glistened along her cheekbone was like a siren's call, beckoning him to his doom.

He didn't think he'd ever been so fiercely attracted to a woman in his life, but at the same time, that attraction didn't matter nearly as much as the calming sort of presence she had over his mind.

But that shouldn't matter, *couldn't* matter. It wasn't her job as a woman to fix a broken man.

And yet she stayed. Even when her lunch was over. Even though she knew she could get in trouble. She stayed.

For him.

It just didn't make sense. She didn't know him. He had hurt her. For all intents and purposes, she should be running for the hills. And now that he had asked her such a monumentally *stupid* question, he was sure that she finally would.

Which was well enough. He didn't really deserve comfort. There were veterans who lost their legs, or vision, or worse in war. What excuse did he have to be so messed up? He came out unscathed when so many better, stronger men hadn't. None of it was fair.

Something in her face snapped, and she suddenly pulled herself together. "I thought we were trying to keep our knowing each other secret," she said flatly. Not accusingly, not even scared. That was a good thing, right? It gave him a little bit of hope that she wasn't about to shut him out—even if that was exactly what she should do.

"Yeah, that was the plan. But it's not fair that you're doing so much for me and I'm doing nothing for you. So at least let me start with one of Ma's homecooked meals."

"I don't do nice things for people to *get* something out of it."

"I know, I know." He sighed. He really was making a mess of things, so he might as well give up. It was a stupid idea anyway. "Thank you, for spending the afternoon with me."

"Of course. I said I'd help, and I meant it."

The two of them stood, and he helped her to her feet. Her hand felt so small in his, much of her flesh covered up by band-aids. "New callouses?" he asked, looking down at their hands grasped together.

"Yeah, still breaking my hands in."

"I don't know if anyone told you, but vitamin E oil will help a whole bunch with that."

"Thanks."

They took a couple of steps down the knoll before she sighed.

"I'll go to dinner with your family."

More guilt trickled through him. She was only agreeing because she felt obligated. He hated that. "You really don't have to. It was a terrible suggestion."

"It's too late," she said primly, her shoulders squaring. "You made me miss lunch, and now I'm ravenous, so you gotta feed me."

She was... far too good for him. Relief rushed through him, and he thanked God for the strange circumstances under which they met. "That sounds fair enough to me."

"Good. Glad to know my logic works out."

The conversation sort of lulled as they walked toward the main house, their feet moving over the grass a bit too quickly. Now he was beginning to doubt himself and his silly little request.

"So, what's our story?" Missy asked when they were nearing the house but were still far enough away not to be overheard.

"What do you mean?"

"Well, I'm pretty against the idea of telling my bosses that I snuck onto their property and surprised one of their sons when he was in a medical crisis. And you don't seem so keen on them knowing that either, so I think a cover story would be apt."

"The way you say it, it makes you sound like the guilty party here."

She shrugged, the sun glinting off her golden shoulders as if it wanted to emphasize the action. "I mean, none of this would have happened if I wasn't kinda fudging the rules to see some stars."

But thank God she did. It made his stomach churn how quickly his view of her was shifting, and how attached he was already, but he supposed there was nothing else that he could do. She was the first person who he didn't feel on edge around since he got back, even if he didn't know why.

Missy's face lit up suddenly. "Oh! I know! How about you helped me with the kitten I found in the barn, and we got to talking about animals? Would they buy that?"

"I... suppose. I've always had a soft spot for felines."

"Really?"

He nodded. "Yeah, a lot of the barn cats used to follow me around, and I just sort of understood them in a way. They're funny creatures. Trying to pretend that they're aloof when they're some of the cuddliest, most loving animals."

The smile she sent him was nearly dazzling, and he almost missed a step. "You're the first person I've talked to that *gets* that! So many people have this idea that cats are these emotionless jerks, but they only act that way at first because they have to figure you out. You prove your trustworthiness to a cat, they're your friend for life."

Huh.

The compassion in her voice was intimidating but almost inspiring in a way. If she felt so strongly about animals, enough to make her whole face illuminate with joy, he was maybe starting to understand why she could treat him so graciously.

They finally reached the front of the house. It felt different than when they had been there the previous night—which made sense—but now he found himself looking up at the meticulously built home and almost felt intimidated himself.

"It's not too late to back out," he said to her, noting the color that drained from her face.

"No, I—"

Before she could get the words out, the door flung open and

Ma was standing right there, her face flushed and a smile in place.

"Bartie! You've been out all day—" she trailed off when she saw the woman next to him and slipped into her normal, hospitality mode. "Oh, it's the young lady from town I hired." She smiled warmly. "What can I help you with, dear?"

"Hi, Mrs. Miller, I, uh, I was—"

He didn't think that he would ever see Missy speechless. So far, his interactions with her involved her being endlessly confident or blithe. It was a bit bizarre to see her so shaken by his mother.

Not that Mrs. Miller wasn't a force to be reckoned with, but she used her power very selectively.

"I asked her to dinner, Ma. I hope you don't mind." He walked up the stairs and pressed a kiss to the older woman's cheek.

"You did?" The surprise in the woman's tone was clear. He didn't take offense to it, however. Him inviting someone to dinner meant he actually talked to someone of his own volition, and that in and of itself was pretty shocking.

"Yeah. She rescued a little barn kitten. We got to talking about cats."

"And so you invited her to dinner?"

He shrugged, once again borrowing a play from Missy's book. "Yes."

"All right, well come on in then. I made something summery, I hope y'all are in the mood."

"From what Bart says about your cooking, I can't imagine I wouldn't be in the mood," Missy said politely, following Ma's gesture to walk in.

"Oh, so you talked about my cooking?" Ma asked, raising an eyebrow as he followed after Missy.

He had just complicated things, hadn't he? But how bad could it be? He had survived a whole war after all.

Then again, he had come out of that war with a broken mind and nightmares that bled into the waking world.

Huh. Maybe this wasn't a good idea after all.

He supposed there was only one way to find out.

15

———————

Missy

$\mathcal{M}$issy looked over the large table at the faces staring at her, all with a mix of curiosity and confusion. It took all of her power to keep her expression in one of passive friendliness when really, she just wanted to slide off her chair and crawl out the door.

This was awful.

This was terrible.

This was why one avoided socializing with one's employers whenever one could.

But for some reason, she had agreed to Bart's request, and now she had a whole horde of *them* staring her down and only one of her.

But when her gaze flicked to Bart, he gave her a grateful sort of look that told her she was doing the right thing. And, like usual, the right thing wasn't comfortable.

"This is one of our workers," Mrs. Miller said, explaining Missy's presence. Most of the food was already on the table, smelling delicious and way more inviting than the stares Missy could feel on her skin. "Bartie, why don't you introduce her?"

"Uh, all right."

Missy watched as he swallowed, feeling her own stomach twist a bit. She got the impression that he wasn't really a fan of public speaking, even if the public was just five people around the dinner table.

"This is Melissa Dominic—"

"Please, call me Missy," she interjected, trying to smile softly. She knew how to navigate situations like this, she just so rarely had a chance to. Usually, when she walked into a room, people had already made their assumptions about her. Unlike most movie protagonists, her reputation almost always proceeded her.

"Right. Missy." Bart pointed to the closest man, a dad-looking type with salt and pepper to his beard. "This is cousin Afton. He's visiting from St. Louis."

"Hello," she replied automatically.

"And this is Bradley, my younger brother."

Bradley tipped his head toward her. "Pleased to meet you again, ma'am. Your supervisor has nothing but praises about you."

Missy flushed at that. She owed a lot to the Millers and was pleased to hear that she was proving herself as a hard worker. "Thank you."

"And this is Pa."

The white-haired man nodded to her, his incredibly tanned

face impassive. He had deep-set wrinkles in his visage, the ones that spoke of decades of hard work and wisdom. She bet that she could learn a whole lot from him.

In a hypothetical world, of course. Because she hoped that she would never have to see these people again. Helping Bart was one thing, but she had no intentions of getting chummy-chummy with the rest of his rich family. That was just asking for trouble. She could already hear the whispers of gold digger and the accusations of her employment being some sort of long con.

Maybe that was just her paranoia. Maybe not everyone thought such cruel things about her. But if life had taught her one thing, it was that she shouldn't take the chance and give anyone the benefit of the doubt.

"And I'm assuming you've met Ma since she was the one who hired you, and well... I'm me."

"Yes, you are you," Missy said with a wry smile.

"Thank you, Bartie," Mrs. Miller said, her smile so kind and sweet that Missy was beginning to get why her sons were so endearing. There was a sort of light to the woman. Would her mom have been the same way now, if she had lived? Missy assumed the two women were similar in age. Would they have been friends?

She felt the familiar sensation of tears trying to wheedle into the corner of her eyes, and she blinked them away. This was not the time to let thoughts of her mother sidetrack her. It had been years, after all, and she had certainly dealt with her grief many times over.

"Let's say grace."

Missy startled when Bart offered her his hand on one of her sides and Bradley on the other. She looked to them in concern before putting two and two together and sliding her palms above theirs.

Normally she avoided touch. It either encouraged situations she didn't want, or rumors about her character. But she couldn't help but feel a strange sense of connectedness as everyone bowed their heads.

Was this what it felt like to have a normal family? One where people ate meals together and sent words to God? One where the first course of a dinner wasn't beer followed by a liquor chaser?

The prayer was over too fast for her to really figure out if she liked the thumping of her heart or not, and then suddenly everyone was passing the food around.

And *boy* was it a lot of food.

Missy was a healthy woman, one who rarely skipped a meal and loved her red meat and potatoes, but her budget wasn't nearly able to keep up with her appetite. Often, she relied on meals of rice and hot sauce or multiple packets of ramen. But it was clear the Millers didn't have any problems keeping their table full of quality ingredients.

They had a whole platter of grilled pineapple chicken, glazed and covered with a generous portion of fruit. There was also a delicious summer salad filled with fresh vegetables, and wine on the table along with a large pitcher of fresh water. What was essentially a full feast for her was a normal Tuesday dinner for them.

Boy, rich people were a trip.

"This is delicious," Missy said, barely restraining herself from ripping into the drumstick on her plate with her teeth. The last thing she wanted to look like was a barbarian in front of her bosses. She wished she wasn't dressed in grungy overalls and a tank top in front of the people who paid her.

"I'm so glad you like it," Mrs. Miller said with a smile. Just barely at the end, Missy caught the older woman's eyes flick to her neck, where the blue bandana set. She felt herself blush a bit and looked back down at the plate.

She very much doubted that Mrs. Miller would guess what had happened, but she also didn't want the woman to get any other ideas. Hopefully, she would just let it go as a hickey or some other abrasion. The bandana covered up most of it since she was sitting still and not raking out multiple cow stalls.

"Yeah, it's amazing. If I had meals like this every day, I don't think I'd be able to fit into my clothes anymore."

"Oh, well I don't know about that," Bradley said with a laugh. "Ranch life is pretty physical work. I've seen a lot of my cousins really put it away and never gain a pound."

"You mean Ben?" Mrs. Miller retorted with a chuckle.

Bart rolled his eyes. "I've seen the guy devour an entire pecan pie after dinner and wake up like he'd been starved for three years."

Missy smiled too, the tiniest of a thrill running through her. She liked seeing Bart snarky. Normal. She knew he'd only been conscious for about half the time they'd spent together, but that little glimpse of normalcy gave her hope that there was a light for him at the end of the tunnel.

"Don't be jealous just because he got the best metabolism out of all of us," Bradley said with a laugh. "I like not having to eat every couple of hours. Remember in high school, when we had to get a doctor's note to let him eat in class because he used to get lightheaded having to wait until he got home?"

Bart chuckled. "Yeah, I remember. At least now he seems to

have somewhat leveled out. I'd hate to think about that new girl of his having to keep up with all that appetite."

"Please, like she'd be that domestic. That girl has way too many ambitions to try to keep up with his dietary needs."

Normally, Missy would take a comment like that as a red flag, but Bradley said it with admiration, not derision. One of the many things she hated about her small town was that often women were expected to only have certain roles. And while she fully supported every woman who wanted to be a domestic goddess, Missy didn't like that it was treated as a matter of course. Just like men, some women flourished in a caretaking role, and sometimes they needed something different.

Like her.

She needed something more, but she didn't know what. Sometimes, she just wanted to abandon the town that she didn't fit into, pack up and never look back.

But she didn't have the resources to go anywhere else, and the thought of leaving her father and mother alone, their bones never visited, their graves left without flowers, made her stomach twist. They were all she had, and even if they were dead, she still didn't want to leave them.

"Speaking of ambitions," Mrs. Miller said. "Are you looking at getting back into the veterinary field, or have you fallen in love with ranch life?"

Missy quickly chewed the mouthful she had bitten off. She had been hoping that they might let her slip by without much conversation, but it seemed that was not her luck.

"I just got here, really," she said with what she hoped was a polite smile. "Think I'll stick around for a while and learn what I can before I start looking for new work."

"We look forward to having you here," Bradley said with a warm smile.

Geez, the Miller boys really were a pretty crew, weren't they? It didn't seem quite fair. But the nice feeling she had from his easy welcome faded when her eyes flicked to Mrs. Miller, and she saw... something there that she couldn't place. Dropping her eyes down to her plate, she resolved to eat as quickly as she could before escaping and getting back home. Goodness knew her pets were probably missing her.

MISSY WAS STUFFED. So pleasantly full that if she was home, she would have popped the button of her jeans and let her soft stomach expand how it wanted too. But she definitely wasn't home, and she was also wearing overalls, so she contented herself with sitting back in her chair and waiting for a pause where she could exit.

The conversation during the rest of the meal had been fairly innocuous, with Bart sending her grateful or exasperated looks over the table at appropriate times. She was glad that she was there for him; her presence seemed to make him more comfortable for some reason. Maybe it was because he didn't have to pretend with her. She'd seen him at his absolute worst, and it hadn't scared her off.

He would have to do something purposely bad to her to do that. Once, when she was seventeen, she had come across a desert owl caught up in some discarded tangle of plastic, most likely something left over from the temporary barriers set up for the town's yearly marathon. She'd only had her car keys on her, but she had dutifully worked to free the guy.

He wasn't happy, and she couldn't really blame him. He was in a compromising position, and she was a big ol' predator. He had tried to attack her repeatedly, his claws cutting so deep into her arm that she ended up needing stitches. She still had the scars to this day, silvery little lines to remember him by.

So yeah, if he thought he was the first terrified creature fighting for his life that she'd dealt with, he was wrong.

"Thank you so much for the meal," Missy said finally, pushing herself back from the table. "But my little ones are probably wondering where I am."

Mrs. Miller's head rotated to look at her. "Oh, you have children?"

Missy couldn't help it, she snorted at the absurdity of that idea. She was pretty sure that she was missing one of the vital steps in childbearing. Or basically all of them. "Goodness no. I mean my rescue animals."

Mrs. Miller's smile was a bit embarrassed. "Oh, I see. Apologies for assuming."

Missy waved it away with her hand. "Don't worry about it, I can see how my wording was confusing. I guess sometimes it feels like they *are* my children, hah."

"Nothing wrong with having compassion for God's loving creations." Bart's mother stood, wiping off her apron. The thing was quite pretty, and Missy couldn't help but wonder if the woman had made it herself.

"Bartie, Bradley, would you mind clearing the table? I'll walk our guest to her car."

Bart looked startled at that. "Uh, I can do that Ma. I invited her, after all."

"Nonsense," Mrs. Miller said breezily. "It's not often that I get to spend time with another lady." She sniffed her nose dramatically. "It's a wonder I don't go insane from all the testosterone around here, I tell ya."

"See," Bradley hissed conspiratorially to his brother but loud enough for everyone to hear. "I told you she always wanted Bryant to be a girl."

"Please," their father retorted, probably the first time he had spoken the whole meal. "Not with the way he cats around town. The last thing we'd need is our only daughter having that kind of reputation."

Missy stiffened at that, fighting to keep her expression neutral. So they were somewhat at peace with their youngest being a player? But couldn't stand the idea of a daughter doing the same? It was a hypocrisy Missy had run into plenty of times in her life, but she didn't expect to find it here.

Oh well. It wasn't like she'd be seeing these people very often. From now on, she had to keep her head low and work, work, work.

"Let me pack you up a meal to go," Mrs. Miller said chipperly before disappearing to the kitchen before Missy could protest.

Not that she would really mean her protests. The food was *really* good.

But even with that extra step, it wasn't long before Mrs. Miller was linking her arm through Missy's and they were both walking to her truck.

It seemed like an entirely different day since she'd come into work, her body and mind were exhausted from being out so late the day previous. Now that she knew she would be back to her bed soon, her weariness was starting to come back with a vengeance.

"You can keep the basket and Tupperware, dear," Mrs. Miller

said on the way to their destination, still as sweet as pie. "I have so many of them, sometimes I don't know what to do with it all! I try not to hoard things, but with five sons, I never seem to be able to find the balance of what is just enough leftover containers and what's just short."

Missy laughed, having finally reached her car. She disentangled herself from the matriarch and gave her what she hoped was a very grateful smile. "Thank you so much for the lovely meal. Really. I can't thank you enough."

"Of course, dear, my door is always open to anyone who's hungry."

"That's real charitable of you ma'am."

The whole thing ended a lot nicer than Missy had ever expected, and she pulled her keys from her pocket, sliding them into the keyhole. But before she could open her door, Mrs. Miller was talking again.

She should have known better.

"Before you go, may I ask about the bruises around your neck?"

Missy flushed with embarrassment. Slowly, Missy turned away from the car and gave the woman a patient smile. She didn't want to lie to Mrs. Miller, but at the same time she had promised Bart she wouldn't tell.

"Oh, it's nothing," Missy said, hoping Mrs. Miller would drop the subject.

Mrs. Miller reached out her hand and touched Missy's arm. "I think it is something. And I want to help. You can tell me. It'll be okay."

"I'm sorry Mrs. Miller. I can't tell you. I promised."

"I invited you to work here because I saw that you were really trying to provide for yourself, and I felt sorry that no one was willing to give you a chance. The bruises on your neck tell me that something dangerous might be going on."

"Oh, it's not like that at all," Missy said, her eyes wide at the insinuation.

"Whatever it is, I'm concerned how it might affect Bart. You are aware, I'm sure, that he is having a tough go of it right now. He isn't the most... social of my sons, so it certainly was quite a surprise for him to invite you to dinner."

Missy's eyes narrowed as she thought she heard suspicion hidden within the polite overtones. "Yeah, it surprised me too," Missy said flatly. "Your son is the one who invited me to dinner, ma'am. I didn't ask."

Mrs. Miller was still staring at her expectantly. "I don't want Bart to get hurt. And I'm not sure he understands what's real and what isn't."

It was clear that the woman had already made up her mind about Missy, assuming the same things everyone else assumed. Missy had thought that the ranch was different, that this would be a place to get away from all that.

But she'd been wrong. Like she usually was.

Missy opened her mouth to defend herself, because she had never *asked* the woman to take pity on her, but Mrs. Miller kept right on going.

"Do you think you are equipped to handle him with extreme care and patience? This might not be the best time for him to get attached to someone. And definitely not a good time for a fling. Most of all, I don't want to see his heart broken."

Missy heard the innuendo behind the words Mrs. Miller was saying. Just because her parents died and her dad had been a drunk, didn't mean she wasn't a caring person. Just because she was stacked didn't mean she went around seducing people for a good time. Missy felt her temper rise, but it was nothing compared to the sinking feeling in her soul.

She had thought this place was safe. That it would be good for her.

Was any place ever going to be right for her? Or was this just her life forever?

Missy looked up at Mrs. Miller, feeling defeated. When Missy spoke, there was no bite to her voice, just weariness. *Ugh.* She hated sounding weak! It let people know that they got to her. That she let their words color her perception of herself.

"Do I really seem like the kind of person to just have a fling?" she whispered. "To go around throwing myself at men and using them?" She couldn't help it. She wanted to know. She figured Mrs. Miller was old enough and wise enough to be an excellent judge of character, so what did it mean if she looked Missy over and only saw trash?

Mrs. Miller hesitated for a moment. "I would like to think the best of everyone and say no. I'm just trying to protect my son."

What a polite way to say yes.

The world was swirling around Missy, cold and harsh and unwelcoming. Carefully, she took a long breath before speaking again. "I think, if you are so uncertain of my character, then perhaps this isn't the right place for me after all."

Mrs. Miller opened her mouth to speak again, but Missy was done with it. She knew how these things always turned out, and it was with her being the bad guy, the succubus, while everyone else around her were pious saints who managed to withstand her corruption.

Without another word, her hand went to truck's door and

she clambered in. Quick as she could, she started her engine and pulled out.

The farther she got, the more her anger grew, pushing past the self-loathing and shame. All of this just because she tried to help a guy who was in pain. Who needed someone outside of his family to tell him that there was hope.

She liked to think that she finally learned her lesson; she needed to stop sticking her neck out for people who were all too happy to put her on the guillotine. But as the anger faded, leaving her empty and hollow, she knew that wasn't very likely. She didn't think she could ever sit idly by and watch someone struggle when she might be able to make their burden a little lighter.

Even if it hurt her every time.

16

Bart

𝒲hen Bart opened his eyes again, he was surprised to feel the same pleasantness as the day before. No fatigue, no dread for the coming day. Just a sense of being well-rested and willing to accomplish things.

Huh.

He yawned and gave his body one of those satisfying, all over stretches that was both relaxing and invigorating at the same time. Memories from yesterday drifted back to him as he settled into the mattress again, and he couldn't help but get a smile on his face when he thought about Missy.

Dinner last night had been amazing.

Actually, the whole second half of the day had been amazing. Talking to Missy had been like releasing some sort of catalyst in him, one that made the constant noise in the back of his head seem more bearable.

He couldn't put his finger on the why or how of it considering none of it made sense. After all, he had his brothers and parents and therapist to talk to. He loved them all dearly and trusted them more than anything. He wouldn't even be alive now if it weren't for them.

And yet, it was the strange woman who liked to stare up at the stars that finally eased the maelstrom.

He didn't know if perhaps it was how she looked at him, like he was human instead of some ticking time bomb ready to go off. Because even *he* viewed himself that way. He didn't know if it was the way her head tilted back when she gave a good laugh, her full lips parting into a smile that made it seem like nothing could go wrong. He didn't know if it was the effervescence she exuded, or the sarcasm and wit that was always catching him off guard, or even her glib sort of randomness when she would go from discussing the light spectrum to her favorite acronyms, or the fact that koalas spent most of their lives drunk on eucalyptus leaves.

Whatever it was, it was working for him.

Whistling to himself, Bart set out for another day of helping his brothers. Ben was still gone, but Benji had arrived a bit after dinner, swinging by to say "hi" before heading to his own bachelor cabin. Bradley was grateful to be back on the books side of things, but Bart was eager to use his hands for something.

As long as it wasn't with the same men from yesterday. Although Missy had soothed the red out of his vision, he didn't want a relapse by being reintroduced to the crass young men who had triggered him.

Besides, anyone who could talk so rudely about Missy, or any woman for that matter, was no friend of his.

He hit the shower and got dressed, but this time as he passed the steamed mirror in the room, he paused to wipe it off. Nothing wrong with gussying himself up a little.

He looked at his hair. It had certainly grown out quite a bit in the time that he'd been home. Looked like he was due for a trim. He just hadn't thought about it. Maybe it was time to start thinking about things like that.

But he didn't want to take a pair of scissors to it at the moment, so he did the best he could at brushing it into a somewhat presentable style and then headed to his closet.

He looked over the clothes that he had never paid much attention to. For being a man in his thirties, he supposed his Ma shouldn't be buying most of his clothes. Then again, considering that most of their stuff was ordered from some sort of fancy catalog, he wondered if Bradley had set up a recurring order. Seemed like something he'd do.

Maybe he should take a trip to the city and get something better. Something that made it look like he was trying.

But what exactly was he trying for?

He shoved that thought down and instead picked out a simple work shirt, a white undershirt and one of his toughest pairs of jeans that didn't have hard-set stains in them. He couldn't remember the last time that he had cared about how he looked. Probably before the military.

Whatever. It didn't matter. The important thing was that he was feeling good for once and ready to tackle the day. And twice in a row? That was a gift that he wasn't going to look at twice.

With a strange sort of churning in his stomach, he headed out to help Benji.

But on his way to the outer edge of things, where the middle brother would undoubtedly be working, he took a last-minute detour. Before he could really figure it out, he was standing in front of the barn, watching the barn-hands do their thing.

Wait.

Was he really doing this?

This seemed like probably the last thing she would want, but then he was walking forward.

He worked a circuit around the place, not sure where her assigned stalls for the day would be. She wasn't in any of them, so he figured maybe she was grabbing some water or even just relieving herself. Goodness knew it was about a five-minute walk to the closest bathroom station they had.

Back when he was younger, they just had outhouses, but Ben had insisted that, as their land grew, they install actual working bathrooms around the place. They were little bits of luxury the family could more than afford, so by the time he was a teenager, they dotted the entire property.

Well, he was nothing if not patient. Shrugging his shoulders to himself, Bart went back to finding his brother.

Unlike Bradley, he found Benji working his way inward like he or Ben always did.

"Oh, hey there Bart. Didn't expect you out this early."

"Yeah, I'm trying something new." That seemed the easiest way to explain it. Because meeting a woman and almost killing said woman and then quickly becoming strangely obsessed with said woman was a bit of a mouthful.

If he was being honest with himself, he probably knew that it might be unhealthy how quickly his mind was turning to thoughts about Missy. But it soured his mood when he tried not to think about her, and for once he wanted to enjoy the levity inside of him.

"Huh, that's all right then. You here to help?"

"Yeah, you got work that needs to be done today?"

"When isn't there work?" he replied breezily. Typical Benji. Being the middle child, he really was the most laid back out of all of them. If Bart's temperament was a bit more like his younger brother's, maybe he wouldn't be so fractured now. "Come on, I've still got two-thirds of the checklist left to do."

"Sounds good to me."

The morning passed quickly, with Bart helping here and there. Sheep needed to be sheered, and one of their tractors needed to have its brake lines replaced. Nothing that he could do on his own, but he knew how to assist.

But then lunch was coming around, and he headed back to the barn.

She wasn't there again.

Bart looked around, his brows furrowing. Had she already gone to lunch? He knew their meal hours were flexible, but...

"Hey, can I help you?"

Bart turned to see one of the senior workers at the ranch. Technically, he had been there long enough that he could have any job he wanted, but he chose the manual one. Bart didn't really know why, but he'd never thought to ask.

"Yeah. One of your workers here. She uh, dropped something near the main house. I wanted to return it to her." He internally begged that the man didn't ask what it was because Bart was uncomfortable with lying.

"Oh, you mean Miss Dominic?"

"Is that her name?" Bart said, shuffling. "Almost six feet, blond hair?"

"Yeah, that's her," the worker said with a smile. "She's not here today."

"Ah." Of course. While he knew most of the workers had Sunday off, they all rotated what other days they rested. Most of them chose to work ten-hour days so they could have three off, but he wasn't really up-to-date on their schedules. "Right. Well, just tell her that I'd like to see her if she gets a moment."

"Of course. Hopefully it wasn't too important, whatever she dropped."

"Uh, yeah."

And that was that. Feeling a vague sense of disappointment, he went back to work.

Oh well. There was always tomorrow.

THE NEXT DAY, Bart looked around the barn, a familiar feeling of disappointment again. He'd woken up in a good mood and determined to successfully ask Missy to dinner, only to find that she wasn't where she was supposed to be.

He knew that she could just be on another day off, or even running late, but something didn't sit easy in his stomach.

He looked to the other workers, wondering if he should ask about her, but he didn't want to show too much interest and raise people's suspicions. Not that he was worried about what they thought of him—at least not at the moment—but he didn't want gossip to turn against *her*. Missy seemed pretty concerned with what people said about her, and even though he wasn't sure it was necessary, he respected her caution.

But he was so *impatient*. It was like someone had opened a door, giving him a peek of what was just beyond, then slammed it right back in his face. He could feel the anxiety setting in, whispering things that he didn't want to hear, and the little surprise noises that come hand-in-hand with ranch life were startling enough to make him feel sick.

Feeling more than a bit put out, he headed back to the edge of the farm. There he saw Benji, Bradley, *and* Ben, all of them catching up.

"What's this? Someone called for a brother's meet-up and didn't invite me?" he cracked. Wow. He almost sounded like the old Bart there. That was something new.

"Three days in a row?" Bradley asked teasingly. "What is this, some sort of Christmas in July miracle?"

"Bartie! Good to see you!" Ben crossed over to him and pulled him into a hug. Bart bristled for a moment, adrenaline shooting through him and telling him that someone was trying to hurt him, but he shoved it down and let himself enjoy the embrace.

"Good to see you, too. You were gone long enough with that lady friend of yours."

"Lady friend?" Ben repeated dubiously. "What are we... in high school again?"

"No, but are you guys putting a label on it already?" Benji asked, clapping Ben on the shoulder as he broke away from Bart.

"Already? What do you mean by that? It's basically been an entire decade."

"Yeah, where you didn't talk to each other or have any contact."

"Fair enough," Ben conceded, hands raised. "Sorry, I took a couple of extra days. It's not often Chastity and I get to have time to ourselves and do whatever we want. I guess I got a little carried away with the freedom."

"Uh-huh, I'm sure," Benji said, smirking the way he did when he was razzing his brothers. Bart let the two of them banter about and sidled up beside Bradley, who still had his morning cup of coffee in his hand.

"Hey, got a question for you."

"It better involve the finances because if I have to remember the proper way to start a cattle drive again, I might just pitch myself off a cliff."

"It's just a personnel question."

Bradley sighed happily as he took another long swig of coffee. "Now that...I'm good with. What's up? Finally gonna file a complaint about those guys who riled you up?"

"How do you know about that?"

"I'm the books guy, I know about a lot."

Bart shook his head, not letting that worrying idea distract him. "There's a worker here I wanted to check in on. One of the muckrakers."

"The girl you invited to dinner?" There was something strange about his tone, and Bart guessed that he was being just a touch too direct, but oh well. There was no going back now.

"Yeah, Missy."

"She quit."

The ground dropped out from under Bart, and suddenly he was falling. His body slid past smoke and darkness and screams before he blinked it all away and focused on his breathing.

In.

Out.

In.

Out.

When he was centered enough to speak, he chose his words carefully. "What happened?"

Had she overheard those men talking about her? Had she gotten a better job offer in town? He was foolish to think that she'd stick around just for him. He wasn't anything to her.

Anything at all.

Bradley shrugged. "Dunno. She called in yesterday morning and said she wasn't a good fit. And that was that."

"That was that?" Bart echoed. "You didn't try to talk to her?"

"What did you want me to do?" he asked with a raised brow. "Convince her to stay? You weren't there, Bart, but she sounded pretty adamant. And a woman like that, I don't think you could convince her to change her mind once she's set."

"What do you mean, a woman like that?"

Bradley rolled his eyes. "Don't use that tone with me. You've seen how she walks, how she holds herself. That was a woman who fought for everything she had in life and certainly didn't have anyone give her any handouts. I'm sure she's been looking out for herself for so long that she knows what's best for her way better than I do. So, if she says she wants to quit, I'll let her quit."

Bart hated to admit it, but his younger brother had a point. One of the things he had learned about Missy was that she was fearless. Determined. Very little scared her. If she had wanted to move on, well that was her right, and he should respect that.

...except something didn't quite seem right.

At dinner she had been all smiles, her eyes flicking to his own every once in a while to communicate with him. He knew his family was... different than a lot of others, but she seemed to take it in stride. She'd been charming. And reassuring.

How could they have gone from *that* to her disappearing from his life entirely?

There had to be some piece he was missing.

"You okay, big guy?"

Bart broke free of his thoughts, looking to Bradley, who was eyeing him with concern.

"Yeah. Yeah, I'm fine. There's just something I need to check at the house."

"You sure, man?"

"I'm fine. I promise."

"Okay, if you say so," Bradley said.

Bart went to go, but his brother's hand on his shoulder stopped him.

"Trust me, you didn't scare her off or anything. I'm real proud of you making a friend."

Bart felt his heart squeeze. He really was lucky he had the family he did. They deserved so much better than him.

But he was *trying*.

"Thanks, little bro," he said, ruffling Bradley's hair and heading back to the main house.

When he reached it, he could smell the mouthwatering scent of freshly baked bread wafting from the kitchen. Good, that meant Ma was home. If anyone had an idea of what was up, she would. Ma could read almost anyone like a book. She would know if he had misread Missy's behavior entirely.

Now, how to ask her without setting off any of her all-knowing mother alarms.

"Hey, Ma, do you know what happened with that worker, Melissa Dominic?"

Oh.

That was not the way to do it.

She stood up, a smile plastered across her face and her cheeks red from the heat of the oven. "Bartie! You're up early again. Are you trying a new schedule?"

"Yeah. Lately, I've been feeling more ready to face the day."

"Well, that's wonderful. I'm sure your therapist at the VA will be happy to hear that."

"Yeah, I'm sure. But that's not why I came here. Melissa Dominic, did anything strange happen with her after dinner? Or during?"

A strange expression crossed Ma's face. Why was everyone being so cagey lately? "I'm not quite sure what you mean."

Now that didn't sound like his Ma at all. "I'm just saying, I invited a nice worker of ours to dinner, and everything seemed to be going well, but then she called in the next day and quit. Did I do something wrong? Was I rude at the meal? Did I chew with my mouth open or something?"

None of those sounded like things that would make Missy quit, but his mind was spinning in a panic, trying to figure out what was going on. Just when he was getting his feet underneath himself, they were getting yanked away with no warning. Routine was part of his therapy; it was supposed to keep him grounded and on track, but how was he supposed to have a routine with a mystery woman sweeping into his life then disappearing just as quickly?

"Oh? She quit? How unfortunate."

Bart may have been a man struggling with PTSD and his place in the world, but he knew guilt when he saw it. Narrowing his gaze at his mother, he watched as her eyes tried to flit anywhere but to him.

No.

No.

She wouldn't have....

Would she?

"Ma," Bart said slowly, hoping against all hopes that he was wrong. "Did you *say* something to her?"

17

Missy

Missy closed a tab on her computer, rubbing her eyes before returning to the seven other tabs she had open. Just seven more applications to fill out, then she could take a break.

This time she wasn't wasting her time and looking for jobs in town. It had been made abundantly clear to her that no one wanted to give her work, and she didn't feel like throwing herself at that wall anymore. Maybe in a month or two, she could try the vet's clinic again. They had seemed happy to see her when she dropped the kitten off. And they'd even found someone to adopt it. She was sure that at least one of his children were going to college, and maybe if she took a bit of a pay cut, they would be willing to hire her until the summer.

Even though she had only worked for the Millers for two

weeks, that cash flow had been a massive boom to her. She bet, if she scrimped and saved the rest of the year, she would finally have enough to move to the closest city and rent a studio or a one-bedroom apartment. Sure, she would lose a lot of the space she had now, and her wonderful tub, but she would be free from the town and the vile expectations it had of her.

Or she could just give in.

Missy shook her head at the thought. Sometimes it was tempting to stop fighting against everything and just be the woman that everyone thought she was, but she didn't work that way. She didn't trust people enough for friendship, let alone any romantic feelings. And, unlike some people, she was pretty sure she'd have to have a heck of a whole lot of romantic feelings to let *anyone* see her naked.

She shuddered at the thought. For someone who was pretty confident in her body, she sure hated the idea of ever being that vulnerable in front of someone. Clothing was just another layer to keep people at bay, and as she had recently learned—*again*—she needed to keep people as far away as possible.

She stood up to get a glass of cold water, her window open and both of her fans pointed at her, but she was still hot. Part of scrimping and saving meant not turning on her window-AC unit, which was a huge suck in her energy bill. On her journey, she stopped at the full-length mirror she had bought from the local second-hand store, looking at herself in her shorts and simple tank.

Her eyes traveled over her form, from her large, pale feet, to her shapely tanned legs, to her full hips. She supposed she was what people called "thick" nowadays, but she preferred to think of herself as more of an hourglass.

Continuing upward was her long torso, strong enough to

support her back during hard labor but soft enough to be feminine. Then her bust, which she was well aware was larger than it had any right to be. On top of that were broad, strong shoulders, long muscled arms, and well-worn hands. Hands that worked. Hands that knew what it was like to pave the way for herself.

Finish that off with a slender neck, plump lips, a heart-shaped face and blond, wavy hair, and it was a body anyone should be proud to have. And for the most part, she was. She *liked* how she looked. She didn't think there was anything inherently wrong or sinful about her body. It was just how God made her.

It was just that with so many eyes on her, so many unasked-for gazes and lingering stares, subtle copped feels and not-so-subtle gropes ever since she was fifteen, her body had become not her own. The beautiful vessel that she was in was almost treated as if it was the property of everyone who saw her, instead of herself. Like all of society had ownership of it, and she was only the renter.

She *hated* that feeling, and she had no doubt it colored her ability to have a relationship. And by that, she meant not have a relationship at all. Maybe when she moved, she would have time and energy to open herself up to romance, but she couldn't envision trusting someone like that.

Shaking her head, she removed her gaze from the mirror and got a glass of water. Missy had no idea why she was waxing so poetically about her body. She guessed she always got a little philosophical after these kinds of rejections.

She'd really had hope for the Miller ranch. It sucked to be right about not being able to trust anyone.

Missy sighed, just about to flop back into her seat when the buzzer by the door sounded. Surprised, she headed to her door and pressed the button that allowed the speaker to work.

"Hello?" she asked curiously.

"Missy?"

What?

The speakers were such poor quality that there was a chance that she was wrong, but Missy was fairly sure that was Bart on the other side.

What was he doing here?

"Bart?" she asked cautiously. She would be lying if she denied that part of her melancholy was that she wouldn't be seeing the enchanting man again. She had just been getting to know him, and it seemed like they could have been real friends. She hadn't had something like that in so long that it felt like a major loss, even if the whole thing had been just beginning.

"Yeah, it's me. I'm sorry if I'm invading your privacy, but I was hoping that we could talk."

Oh.

Right.

For a moment she had hoped that he was here for *her*. But that wasn't the basis of their short relationship, was it? He was struggling and just needed his fix of good old Missy magic so he could go about his life. He was here for himself, and nothing more.

But... was there anything wrong with that? The whole reason they had ever started talking was to help him—because Missy had a feeling that she could make his burden a little lighter. How could she fault him for asking for the exact kind of help she offered?

"I'll be down in a minute," she said after a moment's hesitation.

She didn't want to throw any real clothes on, but she settled for a very light T-shirt over her tank so she wouldn't have to put on a bra. Putting on anything restrictive in the swelter of her apartment was a torture she just didn't feel like dealing with.

Once she was moderately decent, Missy headed down the stairs. She saw him standing just inside the landing, where the air conditioning from the office floated across the hall.

For the slightest of moments, she was really struck by the vision. He looked like something out of a movie, looking up at the stairs through his slightly too-long hair, brows knit with worry.

He was striking, backlit by the summer sun outside, shadows falling across his strong, masculine features. His broad shoulders tense while his calloused hands stayed in his pockets. He was a juxtaposition of strength and uncertainty. It made Missy want to run to him and soothe her fingers over every bit of concern that covered his face until he was finally at peace, but she caught herself after a step.

Oh.

That was a bit odd, wasn't it? As much as her need to take care of things made her see the handsome man as one of her injured rescues, that certainly wasn't the case. She needed to remember that this was a grown man before her. One who had fought and given up so much for his country only to come back with an injury that wasn't easily healed. He wasn't a kitten, or a fox, or even an owl.

She needed to remember that.

"Can I help you?" she asked, proud of how steady her voice kept.

"Yeah. I mean no. I..." He took a deep breath, collecting himself.

She admired that about him. Obviously, he was uncomfortable being here, in town with so many people about, but he was calling on tactics to keep himself steady. It meant he was trying, which was more than her father ever did.

"I wanted to apologize for my mother."

Wait, what?

Her eyes widened, and she stared at him like he had just achieved flight. Far too many of their interactions seemed to end up with one of them ogling at the other in shock, but she wasn't sure what sort of reaction she was supposed to have to that kind of statement.

"You wanted to what?"

"I've been looking for you the past two days on the ranch, and when I couldn't find you, I did a little asking around. I was surprised to find out that you quit because last I knew, we'd both had one of the best days either of us had had in a long time. So, after seeking advice from my Ma, I figured out she may have had something to do with it. Then she told me everything."

He took a step closer, looking up the stairs at her with such a genuine expression on his face that her heart ached. "There's no excuse for her prying into your business. I know that she thought she was protecting me, but it wasn't right. Even if her motives were right, you could have taken everything she said the wrong way. Please believe me that we do not think bad of you."

Another step and her breath was catching in her throat. This was... an apology? People didn't apologize to her. Ever. It was always her fault. She was always somehow to blame.

"I can't blame you for leaving, but my Ma is terribly upset and ashamed. She wanted me to express her apologies to you, and that's not just me blowing it up your skirt. Even though Ma was being nosey, she's a really good woman and didn't mean to do you wrong. I like having you around, and so do all the barn workers. Even my brother Bradley thinks you're a great addition to the family. If you want to come back to us, you'd be more than welcome."

"I don't know..." What did she do in this sort of situation? It just didn't compute. No one had ever come up to her of their own volition and confessed that they were wrong. That their beloved mother was wrong. What was happening? Did the world suddenly turn upside down?

"Of course, we don't expect to get off scot-free. The Miller family did wrong by you, and we're intent on making that right. Ma thought a raise might do, and paid time off for the rest of this week so you can get some rest before coming back."

"Your Ma thought of that?"

He shrugged. "The paid time off might have been my idea. I know I always need a little space after a throw down."

"That's one way of putting it." Was her brain shorting out? She really didn't get all of this. There were too many thoughts and questions all crammed into her mind at once. "I'd like to think about it, if that's all right. Could I tell you in the morning?"

His eyebrows shot up to his thick hairline as if he was surprised that she was giving him a chance. "Uh, yeah. Of course. Take all the time you need." He reached into several pockets before pulling out a small notebook and a pen. Quickly, he jotted something down and handed it to her. "That's my number. You know, for whatever you decide."

"Cool..."

Wow, it was awkward, but she didn't quite know what to do. She had already closed the door on the Miller Ranch, but now this handsome, broken man was standing in front of her, wanting her to come back. It was impossible. It didn't make any sense. And yet there he was.

"I guess I should go. It was nice to see you, Missy."

She noted how his eyes stayed on her face, never slipping to her legs or her chest or any of the other places where people's gazes liked to linger.

"It was nice to see you too, Bart."

He tipped his head, and she swore she saw a bit of a blush on his cheeks as he turned to leave. Then her mouth was opening before her mind caught up, and she heard her own voice call out.

"Bart, wait!"

He turned, very obviously trying to school his features into a nonchalant expression and only succeeding partially. "Yeah?"

"Thank you."

"For what? It's just what's right."

She shook her head. "For caring enough to apologize. It means a lot."

He narrowed his eyes, licking his lips like he was trying to think of what to say next. Missy was lying if her eyes weren't drawn to his kissable mouth, and she found herself wondering what it would be like to press her own lips against his.

"Not nearly as much as you mean to me."

And then he was gone.

She stared after him, watching until he was out of sight, and then it was like the world rushed back to her.

"Whoa," she said to herself. Did he really just say that to her? *Not nearly as much as you mean to me?*

She made it up the stairs, her mind somehow even more full than it had been before. She'd never really been into kissing. Something about someone pressing their chewing and eating organ against her chewing and eating organ while breathing all over her face just seemed gross. But with Bart... she bet it would be different.

Missy shook her head, shooing those thoughts away. He came to apologize to her because he was an amazing man trying to recover from the awful illness that made the world all-too slippery for him. That was it.

But as she wandered over to her computer, she couldn't help but wonder if maybe, just maybe, he could be the kind of guy that she could trust.

Consciousness came to her slowly, her dreams full of questions and a sort of unsettled feeling that left her groggy. She hadn't come to much of a conclusion, and the light of day wasn't welcome yet.

Swinging her legs over the side of the bed, she rubbed her chin. Was she debating because this was actually a hard decision or was she just struggling because her natural inclination to not trust people told her to run far away?

If she was completely honest with herself, she would probably say it was the latter. Which meant that she was letting fear control her, which was something she never wanted to do.

Besides, she thought about never talking to Bart again, and that made her stomach twist a bit. She knew he had plenty of support on his own, but she couldn't help but want to be there for him.

Curious.

But she guessed she knew her answer then.

Feeling around for her phone on the floor where she had left it charging, she pulled it up and scrolled to his number. She'd programmed it into her phone the moment she was back in her apartment after talking with Bart.

Yet even with all her confidence, she found her hands shaking as she dialed each digit. It rang once, then she heard it quickly answered. For a beat, she almost hung up, but the stronger part of her placed it against her ear.

"Missy?"

It was Bart's voice on the other line. Because who else would it be? He sounded somewhere between nervous and relieved, which did funny things to her blood pressure.

"Yeah. It's me."

"Ah. Yes, I figured it would be. Not a lot of people call me."

"I hope I didn't wake you." What was she doing? She was getting sidetracked in what should be a really simple conversation.

"No. I didn't get a lot of sleep, so I was already up."

"Oh, that's not good."

"It's fine. It's the weekend, so I'll have plenty of time to nap."

"Really? You don't seem like the napping type."

He laughed softly, and the sound made goosebumps rise along her arms. "I guess not." There was another one of those awkward silences before he spoke again. "So, did you come to a decision?"

"Straight to the point, aren't you?"

"Let's just say, the anticipation is killing me."

"Fair, fair." She took a deep breath. Enough stalling. "I think I'd like to come back."

"There was another pregnant pause. "Just think?"

"All right. I'm certain. I'd like to be back, if you'll have me."

"Of course, we'll have you. That's what the offer was all about."

"Right. Well, I'll see you Monday?"

She could almost hear the smile in his tone. "I'll see you Monday, Missy."

She heard him start to hang up and then her mouth was blurting things again. "If you still ever need my help for anything, let me know."

"Will do, Missy. Enjoy the rest of your time off."

Then he hung up for real, and she was left staring at her wall, feeling a very strange sort of way. Leaning back in her bed, she couldn't help but wonder if she was stupid for having hope that things would be different the second time around.

18

Missy

$\mathcal{M}$issy hummed to herself, the radio so low it was hardly audible as she drove toward the Miller Ranch. The sun was just starting to rise, illuminating her path with gentle hues of orange, pink and lavender. It was like the world was telling her that it was trying to make up for the bad luck it was always heaping on her head.

In a way, she understood why Mrs. Miller said what she did, and Missy might have misunderstood what she was trying to say. But that wasn't why she was going back. No, the reason for that was the sincerity of Bart's apology. Maybe she was a fool—but given such a heartfelt sorry seemed like a good enough reason to give them another chance.

After all, she couldn't list a single person who had ever apologized to her. She thought about all of the rumors she'd overheard in her life, or outright insults. Some of them because of her father. Some of them about her body. Some of them about her stand-offish nature once she wrote someone off. But when Bart looked at her, it was like she could forget all of that. It didn't matter. He just saw a human.

A human that he wanted to talk to. To spend time with. He'd never tried to press a hand to her inappropriately or sneak a fondle. His eyes never lingered in the wrong place for too long. He respected her.

And that was a pretty good feeling.

She pulled up, nerves bubbling in her middle. Sure, she knew Bart was on her side, but everyone else was another question. She knew that her week-long absence had to be noticed. She didn't really have an excuse in place and hoped that no one would ask.

Thankfully, the bruise around her neck was long gone, a figment of the past. She guessed that was one of the upsides to the way everything turned out. It had taken several days for it to disappear, and maybe with it out of sight for so many days, the rest of the workers would forget it ever existed at all.

Smoothing her hair back into her ponytail, she headed toward the barn.

The pitchfork she liked to use was waiting there like she hadn't been gone for days. She put her earbuds in, started her music up, and got to work.

The minutes passed, shifting into an hour, and then two, and she was pleased that no one stopped her to ask any questions. Instead, there were waves and friendly smiles whenever she went to get a drink or go to the bathroom.

It was like everything was normal.

Fantastic.

It seemed like she really had made the right choice after all. She guessed that even nice ladies like Mrs. Miller could make mistakes and hurt people's feelings more than they had meant to.

She just hoped she wouldn't have to see Bart's mom any time soon. Although Missy was letting go of the situation, that didn't mean she wanted to hang out with the matriarch.

The day went by without much incident, her lunch including friendly conversation with the others in the worker's shed. The only difference really was that she was a whole lot sorer after so many days off. Talk about a workout.

At the end of the workday when it was time to clock out, she was almost to the point of a limp. Geez, she really should have stretched. Oh well. At least no one could accuse her of trying to seduce anyone with her uneven gait.

She pulled her keys out as she got close to her truck, ready to go soak in her tub, only to see that there was someone waiting there, leaning against her cab.

"Bart?" she asked, thinking she recognized the familiar set of broad shoulders.

He turned, a grin spreading across his face. Oh wow. A woman could use a warning before he slapped one of those on her.

"Missy! How was your first day back?"

"Grueling," she answered with a laugh. "What's up?"

"I was wondering if, you know, you're not too tired, if you'd possibly like to—"

As much as she liked seeing him all nervous over speaking to her, she liked confident, happy Bart a lot more than the anxious version.

"It's all right, big guy. Take a breath. I'm not going anywhere in a rush."

He smiled gratefully to her, pausing for a moment. "I was hoping that you'd like to come back at night—like you used to."

She raised her eyebrow. "Why?" Last time that hadn't exactly worked out for the best and Bart seemed like the type to still not forgive himself for that.

"Well, because I have a gift for you."

A gift? Her stomach flipped at that. "Couldn't you just give it to me now?"

He nodded, licking his lips again. Did he have any idea how distracting that was? Probably not. She hadn't even known that it was distracting until he'd turned up at her apartment.

"I could. But I—" another breath. "Nights are hard for me. Well, have been hard again since you left. I just thought it would be nice to…"

Missy blushed slightly. She knew what he meant. Their conversations, this strange connection they had, always seemed best when they were alone. When no one was there to judge them for whatever they said or how silly she made the conversation or how loud he laughed.

But still… was it safe? She'd just joined the family again at the ranch, what if someone caught them? She didn't think that anyone would buy that she wasn't up to something nefarious then, no matter how much Bart defended her.

Her eyes flicked up to him, and she saw so much hope, so much uncertainty, how could she say no? Smiling more softly, she gave him a small nod. "Sure. I'll be there."

"Thanks, Missy. For everything."

He looked like he wanted to say something else, or perhaps

do something else, but instead, he turned on his heel and marched back toward the main house.

Missy took a deep breath as he left, her head churning. Goodness, the world just didn't want to slow down, did it?

DESPITE HAVING MADE up her mind, Missy's head had no problem listing off a million and one reasons why meeting Bart after-hours was a bad idea. But she ignored them. She ignored them as she changed into a simple pair of sweats and a T-shirt. She ignored them as she drove out of town. And as she parked. And as she hauled her butt up the same knoll with a blanket over her shoulder. If she knew anything about her conversations with Bart, they usually involved them sitting—or her laying down—on the ground, and she didn't want to get soaked by dew.

Sure enough, he was standing there at the top of the hill, backlit by the moon and stars. It was quite a sight. Looked like one of those cheesy, romance books that her mother would read during her ultimately futile chemo treatments.

But instead of feeling derision at the cheesiness, Missy's heart skipped a beat as she joined him.

"Hey there, soldier," she said loudly, announcing her presence before she got into striking range. It wasn't a good idea to startle people in general, but it was even less of a good idea to do it to someone still struggling with their PTSD.

"Not a soldier anymore," he said, turning to face her.

Missy opened her mouth to say something but was quickly distracted by the long, narrow box in his arms.

Oh.

So, he had meant a *present* present. This wasn't a metaphor for bringing her back to the ranch or giving her more hours or anything. He'd literally gotten her a gift. It was probably the most obvious interpretation of what he had said, and yet she was still surprised.

"Is that for me?" she asked, still waiting for some sort of trick.

"Do you see any other people here who've been grievously wronged by my family and entirely underappreciated by the world?"

Geez, Bart knew how to lay it on when he was lucid, huh? "Well, I don't know about *grievously*," she said, feeling her cheeks color vibrantly. "But please, continue to feed my ego."

He handed her the present, his eyes everywhere but her. "Here," he said, thrusting it into her arms.

"Oh, thanks," she said awkwardly, nearly dropping it but catching the edge of the parcel at the last moment. Actually, it was pretty weighty for being so slender. What could it possibly be?

"Are you gonna open it?"

"Yeah, just let me, uh..." Stuff like this was so much easier in the movies. When her fingers went to the end of the package, there was tape there, and her nails were too blunt and cracked to scratch it up. When she flipped it over, there was tape there too. Along the side... yup, more tape. "Geez, let me, I gotta," her cheeks burned hotter as she brought her teeth to the corner of the package and ripped. There, at least there was a hole now big enough to wiggle her finger in.

"Sorry," Bart said, his face looking as red as hers felt. "I guess I went a bit overboard with the tape."

"Just shows that you were cautious." Finally, she got through the wrapping to what was sealing the package then tore through that too. She was so absorbed in getting to her prize that she didn't realize what she was looking at until her fingers wrapped around it and pulled it out.

"Is... is this a telescope?" she asked breathlessly, staring at the long cylinder in her hand.

"Yeah. I hope you like it. This is one of the reasons I wanted you to meet me at night again."

Like it? Although Missy was more of an amateur in her stargazing, she knew a nice telescope when she saw one. This particular model was at least seven hundred dollars, and that was in used condition on some of the second-hand sites she frequented.

Had he really spent that much money on *her?*

That was impossible. Maybe it was already in his family. Maybe he had no idea how much it was worth.

"I have a gift receipt if you don't like it," he said hurriedly, handing her a folded-up piece of paper.

Well, there went the idea that this was just something that was laying around his house.

"You really didn't have to do this," she said, not knowing what else to say.

Seven hundred dollars.

Seven hundred *freaking* dollars at a *minimum.*

No one had ever done anything like this for her before. The closest she could remember was when her mother rented a bounce house for her fifth birthday. That had been quite the pretty penny then, but still...

"All right, get it together," she whispered to herself. Bart had money, lots of money. Seven hundred dollars to him was like a drop in the bucket. It really wasn't a big deal.

But as much as she told herself that, her heart didn't want to believe it.

"What was that?" Bart asked, looking at her curiously, his gaze far too intense for her.

"Nothing," she said, the words hardly getting past her throat as it tightened. She wondered if anyone ever told him how extraordinarily nice he was. "It's perfect. Thank you, really."

"It's not a big deal," he said, echoing her own thoughts. "Just wanted to show you that—" he cut himself off, fidgeting. "Hey, you brought a blanket. Wanna sit?"

Thank goodness he changed the subject. Missy wasn't sure how much more of the strangeness between them she could endure. Her heart was thundering in her chest like she had just run a race, and her mind kept telling her that she was anticipating something, but she didn't know what. Was this what it was like to have a panic attack? That would be some pretty unfortunate timing.

Luckily, the panic attack didn't come, and instead, she spread out the blanket so she and Bart could sit down. On opposite ends, of course, with their legs crossed and facing each other.

"So..." she said, uncertain how to get this ball rolling. She'd already covered favorite colors, foods, movies, animations styles, and music. Those were really her go-tos whenever she was trying to distract someone from their thoughts. Usually, she used it on crying kids in the clinic who were scared about their furry friends, but she found it worked on adults just as well. "You wanna—"

"I feel like my family is scared of me sometimes. And I can't really blame them because when I think about it, I'm pretty sure I'm scared of myself."

Okay, they were leaping right out there with both feet. Good to know.

"Why are you scared of yourself?" Missy asked gently. She

had her own theories as to why, but she figured if Bart was bringing up the issue, he wanted to say more about it.

His eyes flicked to hers before going back to the ground. "I mean, isn't that obvious? I'm like a bomb, ready to go off at any moment. You experienced that firsthand."

"I did. But it doesn't mean I'm scared of you."

He snorted. "You probably should be."

She wanted to argue with him, but she realized that this was most definitely not the time. "Why do you feel like I should be?"

"I dunno, I thought maybe—"

"Seriously, if you mention that night right now, I will roll you down this hill and into the pond."

There, a tiny little smirk at that. "Fine. I guess it's because... I used to be so in control of things. I was funny. I could make anyone laugh on a dime. I knew how to read people like a book and could navigate any social situation like nobody's business.

"But now, it feels like at any moment I can be ripped away to this dark, dark place where I don't understand anybody and it feels like somebody else is in my body."

"Somebody else?"

His tone grew quieter, but more bitter, a sharp edge to his words like they were bladed weapons ready to hurt him or anyone else who was in their path. "A soldier. Someone who's meant to follow orders and hurt people."

Missy knew it probably wasn't her place to tell a veteran what his service was all about, but it was awful to hear the pain in his voice. "You know, soldiers do way more than just hurt people. They rescue people. They stop others from being hurt."

"Who sold you that idea?" he said with a snort.

"My aunt."

He narrowed his gaze and gave her a healthy amount of side-eye, so she continued.

"Before we moved out here, my mother was pretty close with my dad's sister-in-law. She was a bit younger, but apparently wicked smart. Every now and then she would sit down and tell us about how she came to America."

"She was an immigrant?"

"A refugee. You ever heard about the Kosovo Crisis?"

Bart nodded.

Missy continued, "I was a kid when it was happening. But apparently, US troops went in with NATO and made sure that things were safe enough for the people to return home.

"There'd been so much danger, so much loss, that she and her family couldn't believe they were getting an escort back to their farm. But when they got there, they found it all burned to the ground.

"And you know what those soldiers did? They stayed. They protected her family. Even with phone calls going on between world leaders. They had nothing to gain, but they stayed. And that was what inspired her family to come to America. And guess what? Those same soldiers kept in touch. Helped them get their residency.

"So yeah, I know that your job isn't easy. And that you've had to hurt a lot of people just to be here today. But let's not pretend that you're some agent of evil. You did your best to protect us."

His eyes flicked to her once more, and even in the cover of night, she could see the red rim of his lids. "You think all that of me?"

"I think all that of almost any soldier I meet. I know a lot of people join up because they feel that have no choice, it *is* an amazing economic opportunity for them that they wouldn't otherwise have. And I know others join because they want to be a part of something bigger than themselves. No matter how you shake it, putting your life at risk for your country takes a whole lot out of you."

Silence again as he seemed to digest what she said, but she didn't mind. It didn't feel like he was locking her out or shutting down. Just that he was thinking.

"You know, you aren't like anyone else I've ever met," he said with a sigh.

"Thanks," she shot back, winking. "I take that as a compliment."

"Good. Because it is." He smiled, and it seemed like they were right back to normal. Or at least what maybe could be *their* normal. She supposed that they hadn't known each other long enough to have a routine thoroughly fleshed out yet. But still, even if it was only the fourth time that they'd been alone and conscious, it felt like she'd known him forever.

"You said your mom was close with your aunt until you moved out here. I thought technology was supposed to eliminate that familiar drifting and all."

Missy shrugged, her go-to move. "I guess it's probably the whole dying thing that killed that relationship."

He stiffened at that.

Right. Sometimes Missy forgot that other people didn't deal with their tragedy by trying to sound vaguely sardonic about the whole thing.

"I-I'm sorry," Bart said.

"Don't be." Another shrug. She was probably going to end up with some sort of shoulder problem due to that. "It happened a long time ago. We all have our tragedies."

"I—but..." He chuckled dryly. "I guess you're right. At least you have your dad."

She couldn't help her snort. The poor guy was sticking his foot right down his throat and had no idea. "Nah, he's dead too."

"You've got to be kidding me." Bart groaned, running one of his large hands through his hair.

Briefly, Missy wondered what those calloused fingers would feel like running through her own blond waves, but she quickly dismissed the thought.

Inappropriate.

"Was it some kind of accident that took both your parents?"

"Mom died of cancer. He couldn't get over it and drank himself into an early grave. Leaving little old me all on my lonesome."

"Really, so you've been alone for the past few years?"

"I dunno. I'd hazard saying that I've been alone ever since Mom was gone. I mean, yeah, my dad's body was there, but his soul checked out with hers. Besides, it's not like drunkards are really up on their parenting one-on-one."

"You're incredible," he said, still shaking his head.

She sat up, giving him a teasing look over her shoulder. "What? Just because my family's cursed?"

"Just because I've never met a person who's so fearlessly alive."

"Say what now?" She was a lot of things, and she wasn't a lot of things, but she'd never heard that term used to describe her before.

"I don't know if I can explain it that well," Bart said, looking down at her with far too much going on behind his gaze. "But these things that happen to you, things that some people would use to color their view of the world forever, you just keep moving past them. You won't let anyone, or anything, take your life out of your hands."

Well, that certainly wasn't true. There was a whole host of things she didn't do because of what other people said or thought about her. Bart's compliment was nice, but she wouldn't say it was entirely accurate.

"You're just saying that because you don't really know me. You've just seen all the nice, shiny parts. Just wait a month or two and then all the flaws start showing through."

"What flaws? That you're a great listener and funny?"

Funny, when most guys went to compliment her, it was always something about her body. It was strange to hear someone go off about her personality or... determination to live, whatever the heck that meant. But Missy almost wondered if she kinda liked it.

Boy, the world was really confusing at the moment.

"That I'm needy. And untrusting. And that I get along with animals better than humans. I'm cold and suspicious—"

"Stop with all of that now," Bart said suddenly. "Are those your words, or are they someone else's?"

"Why would that matter?"

"Because you just told me that your father was an alcoholic. I've got several friends at the VA who are struggling with substance abuse, and almost all of them agree the worst of it is how they cut down the people they love in order to feel like they aren't such miserable wastes of men."

"You're not a—"

"Ah-ah, we're talking about you now. Not me. We spend most of our time talking about me because you're that selfless of a person."

"Or it could be that you just talk a lot."

He laughed at that, and she felt a bit of relief. She could do the serious stuff when it was about his PTSD or health. But about her? No thank you.

"Only for you," he said.

"Oh, so I'm just that special?" She laughed with him. Goodness, she could see herself getting used to moments like this, looking up at the night sky with his face over hers, happiness and kindness written all over his expression.

"Yeah, you definitely are."

Something in his tone made the smile melt from her mouth, and she found him leaning closer to her. Oh, her heart was thundering again, and her entire skin felt like it had just been shocked.

There was a tension in the air, but also coiled thick and tight in her belly. She could feel her cheeks flush while her breathing turned shallow.

"I think you might be the most special person I've ever met." His gaze was serious.

"Careful with those kinds of compliments," she rasped, her eyes darting all over his face. She wanted to drink him up in this moment, like it was something from her dreams. *Goodness*, he was pretty. "A girl could get a bi—"

And then, suddenly, her mouth wasn't talking anymore.

But that was probably because Bart's lips were pressed against hers, warm and soft and everything that she had imagined.

The world did one of those things again where it whirled away in a wash of color, and suddenly everything was so intense that she couldn't perceive it all at once. Bart was so close, so warm, his breath on her face. The cool air brushed over the rest of her body, making her want to curl into his fire and never leave.

It was brilliant, it was electric. It was *perfect*.

She let out the tiniest little gasp. If she had known this was what kissing was like, then maybe she wouldn't have been under the misunderstanding that she hated it. Her body was surging with elation and want and a whole lot of disbelief.

Bart seemed to take that as an invitation, and he deepened the kiss. It was thrilling, but she began to feel as if her heart was beating *too* hard and the pleasant heat was turning into a bit of a raging fire. *Geez*, when had it gotten so hot? She felt like she was in a sauna.

Her body seemed to move of its own accord, her arms reaching up to wrap about Bart's broad, muscled shoulders. She could trust him. She *liked* his kiss. There was no need for the panic building up behind the giddy pleas—

One of his hands slipped into her hair, derailing her train of thought as his thick fingers wound into the tresses there, pressing her deeper into the kiss. The other landed on her hip, feather-light, before increasing in pressure as it glided up her form.

Wait.

Things were going too fast. But she just couldn't *think* over the thrum of her own body and the excitement that was trying to short circuit every single part of her brain. She just needed to breathe for a second, to put everything in order and figure out what was what. She just... a second... just a second...

His hand continued, moving up her middle so softly, tentatively, until one of his knuckles ever so barely brushed against the underside of her heaving chest.

No.

Suddenly everyone's words were in her head at once. *Floozy. Easy. Homewrecker. Tramp. Tart.* What kind of woman laid on a blanket in the middle of a field and let her boss' son feel her up?

The change in her was sudden. She went from warm and pliant to stiff and radiating anger. Bart seemed to sense it, pulling away with a confused look on his face, but it wasn't enough space for her.

"Get off!" she snapped, pushing him away.

In all reality, it probably would have taken a lot more force to remove him from her person, but at her angry shout, he whipped back as if he had been shocked.

"What's wrong?" he asked, eyes wide and face flushed as he looked everywhere for danger.

But stupid, *stupid* tears were already welling in Missy's eyes. She was such a *moron*. She had thought that Bart was different from everyone else. That her body hadn't mattered to him. That he either hadn't heard or didn't care about what people said about her.

Just another thing that she was wrong about.

She fought her way to her feet, head still spinning and lips tingling. Part of her wanted to throw herself back in his arms, not caring about her reputation. After all, since everyone was saying it anyway, would it be so bad to give herself over to the first man she might have actually wanted?

But then her pride came sweeping in. No. She hadn't fought for twenty-three years to prove everyone wrong only to give in to some wounded guy with a strong jaw.

"I thought you were different," she wheezed, her throat squeezing like it did every time she was on the verge of tears.

"What? I... did I read that wrong?" He was on his feet too,

looking utterly distraught. "Missy, I'm sorry. I thought I—*crap*! I just—"

She held up her hands, backing away quickly. "*Don't*." She snapped, feelings threatening to overwhelm her. "Just don't. And don't follow me."

He was looking at her with such confusion and heartache that now the tears were coming up in earnest. That wasn't fair! He didn't get to *do* that! He didn't get to look at her like she'd just torn him in two when his lips, and his hands, and everything about him had called up what she had spent so many years shoving away.

Hastily she ran to her car, leaving her blanket behind. He could keep it. And the stupid telescope.

Stupid, stupid, *stupid!*

That was all she could repeat to herself as she started up the car and peeled out. She had thought that the Miller's place was going to be a safe haven. Somewhere she could just be Missy and nobody else. Yet even here, it didn't seem like she'd ever get away.

But she had to. Or otherwise what was the point of any it? She'd be just what her father, what everyone else always said she'd be.

Goodness, she was just so tired.

19

———

Bart

Bart stared up at the ceiling, sleep being as elusive and broken as usual. Or at least since Missy left. He had just gotten her back, and now he had ruined it all over again.

How exactly had that happened?

He went over everything in his head, trying to see where it first started going wrong. He had invited her back to their hill—was it silly to think of the knoll as theirs? Probably. And then he had given her the present.

She had seemed to like it, judging by her scratchy voice and flushed cheeks. He remembered standing there, wanting to make her always look that happy and surprised. He could easily see himself emptying his bank accounts to shower her with astronomy and pet-related things, and he wouldn't miss a dime.

Then they had talked, and he told her some of the things that had haunted him. Some of the things that he didn't even want to confess to himself. And like usual, she took them all in stride.

No, more than that, she excelled.

She had said a lot of nice things, as per usual, but none of it was usual. For some reason, bathed in the moonlight as they had been, everything had seemed so much more intense, more urgent. And after she peeled back enough of her outer walls for him to see a side of her that he hadn't before, he was suddenly kissing her.

It had been... something else. That was for certain.

He hadn't laid his mouth on anyone since before he left, when he had made some decisions as a twenty-two-year-old that his mother probably wouldn't have been proud of. But after six long years, it was so incredibly easy to get pulled under by the want and desire.

Because there had certainly been a whole lot of that. Missy was the most beautiful woman he had ever seen, and her lips had been so soft, and her body so warm and...

"Come on, get it together, Bart."

But was there any getting it together when he had kissed what might have been an angel that God had sent to Earth?

He closed his eyes and groaned, trying not to think of the little gasp that had escaped that perfect mouth of hers, and how soft her hair had been wound around his fingers.

And then there was his other hand. He had meant to slide it around behind her, support her back while he let his mouth tell her everything that he was feeling. It seemed to have a mind of its own, however, and had slid along her warm, soft, feminine body.

It had been heaven, and despite all the passion raging through him, there'd been peace.

He was where he belonged. In Missy's presence, he felt safe. Centered. Like he was really and truly himself.

And then she had ripped herself away, looking at him like he was a monster.

Ugh.

He sat up, holding the side of his head in irritation at himself. Recalling the look on her face, one of absolute horror and shock.

He really was a monster, wasn't he? She had been trying to help him, and he had let himself get carried away. Why would someone like *her* ever want anything to do with *him*. He was broken. He was so messed up in the head that he was depending on the support of a random farm worker just to function. He had *hurt* her. He was insane to think that she could ever be attracted to him.

Ever want to kiss him.

But even as he sat there in his bed, drowning in his shame and guilt, he couldn't help but replay the moment over and over again in his head.

She was just so...

Perfect.

He had to apologize. He had to grovel before her for anything he did wrong. He didn't deserve her friendship, but he couldn't lie about needing it desperately.

He couldn't help but snort at himself a little. He was by no means a small man and was well aware of his own strength, he could disassemble then reassemble his gun with a blindfold. He knew how to engage a foe with that same gun, or hand to hand.

But none of that strength mattered if Missy was going to hate him.

How had this happened? He'd only known her for less than two weeks. How had she managed to completely turn his life upside down?

He didn't know. And he didn't take the time to figure out any answers. Instead, he strode straight toward the barn, his phone telling him that it was just a bit past the start of the workday.

Hundreds of thoughts flitted through his head about how he would convince her that he was sorry. To beg for her forgiveness. None of them seemed right though. All just cloying and weak and messed up. But he had to at least *try*.

When he reached the barn, he could feel his heart thundering like he was back in that dark place again, but as he walked around, he was beginning to realize that all his rushing was for nothing.

She wasn't there.

"If you're looking for Missy, your brother came and got her this morning."

Bart turned to see the same worker who had told him about Missy not being there before. "Are you sure?"

He nodded. "Yup. If'n you're looking for her, just find him."

Bart nodded, not needing to ask which brother he meant since Ben was back, and he rushed to where he guessed Ben might be on his walkaround.

It took a bit to find him, but eventually they met up, and Bart tried to appear nonchalant.

"Hey, Ben—"

"She's being retrained elsewhere."

Bart stopped short, catching up with the quickly uttered sentence. "I'm sorry, what?"

"You're here to ask about the girl, right? She's been trained elsewhere."

"Oh," Bart said slowly. Well, he'd never been very good at subtlety anyways. "Which are—"

"Sorry, that's an employee matter. It's not really something I can discuss."

Now Bart really was staring at his brother. "What are you talking about? I—"

Ben shot him a sharp look. "Just let it go, Bart. She's in another area of the ranch. If you actually care about her, you won't ask."

Bart hadn't been expecting the tone that his brother was taking with him. Had... had Missy told him everything? His stomach squeezed at that and guilt threatened to drown him entirely. "Ben, I—"

"Whatever you're going to say, I don't really need to hear it. Just go back to the main house and stay out of trouble."

Bart opened his mouth to say something but then realized that he had absolutely nothing to say. This was it. Everyone knew now. That he had hurt Missy and then used up her time like some sort of selfish jerkwad, and then kissed her like an idiot.

And now he couldn't even say sorry.

Bart couldn't go to the house again. Not yet. There would be too many staring eyes, and pitying or disappointed looks. He didn't think that he could stand that.

Instead, he just walked.

And walked.

And walked.

A lot of thoughts went through his mind. Some of them bad,

some of them just confused, but he could feel himself walking back toward the worst he'd ever been.

That was pathetic, right? Shoving off the responsibility for his happiness onto some woman he had just met. It wasn't her deal that he had PTSD that liked to manifest in night terrors and sleepwalking.

He wasn't sure how long he was going to walk, but eventually his phone started to ring. Given that no one ever called him, he quickly pulled it from his pocket.

In all honesty, he had been hoping that it was Missy. Instead, he saw the contact ID for his mother. Clearing his throat and trying to get his head on straight, he answered.

"Hey, Ma."

"Hello, son. Are you all right?"

He knew that tone. It was a mom-tone that meant she already knew the answer. "Why are you asking?"

"Can't a mother be worried about her son?"

"Of course. But that's not why you're calling."

"Fair enough. Where are you?"

Bart sighed. "Walking the fields."

"Are you safe?"

There it was. That worry. He hadn't been fooling anyone, had he? "Yeah, Ma. I just need to think."

"Well, I'd like to talk to you. Could you come home? It's just me here."

"I'm not really sure I'm in the right mindset for a lecture right now, Ma. I'm kinda still reaming myself out."

"I'm not going to lecture anyone, dear. I think that maybe I could shed some light on the situation."

Bart felt something between suspicion and curiosity well up in him. "What do you mean?"

"Just come home, please."

She hung up leaving Bart with a choice. He could do what he usually did when he was struggling and keep on walking, or he could go see what his mother had to say. He knew what fresh back-home Bart would do. But wasn't he trying to be better than that man?

Sighing, he put his phone in his pocket and headed back to the main house.

It didn't take him long to get there, and when he did, he found his mother gently swinging on the porch swing, a jug of lemonade and some fresh crackers with what looked like a summery spread next to them.

"Hey, Ma," he said, sitting down next to her. The swinging was a pleasant sensation, almost soothing, but there was still that edge to his mood.

"Hello, Bartie."

"So, you have some light to shed, huh?"

"Yes dear." She poured a cup of lemonade for herself, then him, and then continued swinging for several moments until she finally spoke again.

"The young woman that you asked to dinner—"

"You can say her name, Ma. We don't have to pretend that she's just another worker anymore."

"So, she *is* important to you?" Her voice was gentle as she spoke. Not accusing. Not reproachful. Just curious, like a mother's should be when she heard that her son might be falling in love with someone.

"Yeah, Ma. I'd say that's the case."

"I see." More silence, as she seemed to think. "So, Miss Dominic called me this morning before work and asked if she could speak to me."

Ah. So this was how everyone found out. It figured.

"I was a bit suspicious, but I thought perhaps she was going to confide in me about how she got those bruises on her neck. I feel a bit guilty about asking her before when we barely knew her."

"Look, Ma. Missy's not a bad girl on in trouble."

"Yes. I get that now. You see, she told me that she understood where I was coming from and that you were lucky to have a mother who cared so much for her son. And to prove that she wanted absolutely nothing to do with you, she asked to work somewhere as far from you as possible, where you would never meet. Or talk. Or at least very rarely."

"I see," he echoed his mother's earlier comment.

"But then Ben calls and tells me that you've been looking everywhere for her, and as a mother, I began to put together that maybe she wasn't the one doing any of the pursuing. According to the other workers, she just seems to want to prove she's a good employee."

Her wise eyes searched his face, seeking out the truth, wanting to comfort but also wanting to know exactly what was happening. He could see all of that crossing her face, and for once, the walls within him rolled down for just a bit.

"Would you say that was true, son?"

"Yeah," he said with a long breath.

Then her hands were over him, assuring him as only a mother could. "Why don't you tell me what happened? From the start?"

And so he did.

All of it.

Every moment of it.

Starting from how he had almost choked her to death and ending with that world-changing kiss.

"Oh... oh my goodness," his mother said when he was finally done.

"Yeah. I messed up big time."

"Yeah, yeah you did."

He was a bit surprised to hear her say it so flatly, but he couldn't argue against the truth. He rubbed his face, feeling even more annoyance with himself.

"Oh, my little Bartie—" Only she could get away with calling him that. "You really don't get it, do you?"

He looked up, sighing bitterly. "What? That I'm a complete idiot who completely misinterpreted my situation with a woman who my parents' employ?"

"I don't think you misinterpreted the situation. I think that you don't understand how things are for Missy."

"What, you mean that her employer's son nearly killed her and then came onto her when she was just being a kind person?"

"*No,*" his mother said firmly. "Think about it for a second, son. Think of how things must be from her viewpoint. How the life she's lived might affect how she would interpret your kissing her."

He tilted his head to the side, trying to think. His mother was looking at him expectantly, and he just didn't get it. "I feel like I'm missing something."

"Goodness, Bartie. *Look* at her! She's like a pin-up on legs."

"*Ma!*"

"What?" she said with a bit of exasperation. "It's the truth. God blessed the woman with a body that even a saint would be tempted for. And with a body like that, you have to take into account that people have reduced her to *just* that since she was a young woman."

His eyes widened, it all started to sink in. His mother seemed to see his expression and nodded.

"There you go. Now you're getting it. Just imagine, even since she was sixteen, or fifteen, or fourteen, she's had men trying to get into her pants. And I don't mean as in a second-hand store."

It was incredibly strange to hear his mother speaking so frankly.

She continued, "So, she's had to build up all these protections to make sure she's safe. That no one is going to take advantage of her like that. And even with all her fighting to stay safe, people still label her with actions and a personality based on what they see.

"So when you kissed her—when you did what no doubt hundreds of men have been trying to do since she was young—you triggered her own boundaries in a way.

"I'm sure she was suddenly sure that you were like everyone else who's hurt her. In that moment, even though you might have meant the best, you were telling her that she was exactly what everyone always told her she was."

Bart stared at her, his stomach twisting. That was the last thing he wanted. "Ma, but I *don't* think that. I never even knew that was a thing!"

It made his temper flare. How could people reduce Missy down to just her parts? She was so strong, wise, and hilarious. She was kind as could be, and strange and brilliant all rolled into one.

Of course, she was bang-up gorgeous and beautifully,

maddeningly soft, but that took a back seat to everything else about her.

"I know, darling. I could tell by the way you looked at her. And how you went into town to apologize for my wrongdoing, and how you fought for her. I also see it in how you're excited to face the day now." Her hand reached out, gently caressing the side of his face. "It has been far too long since I have seen you look forward to anything, and if she is the reason for your happiness, then I owe her all my thanks."

"So then what do I do, Ma? How do I fix it?"

"Treat her how you would any other woman you were interested in."

"But... I don't get it. Isn't that what set her off?" He felt so dumb, needing all of this explained to him by his mother like some schoolboy, but he'd had no idea, not even an inkling, that Missy had a certain... reputation. Sure, those farm hands had said some disgusting things about her, but he had guessed that was what young, twenty-somethings did when they wanted to be edgy. He knew his mouth hadn't been the cleanest when he first joined the military.

"No, what set her off was the kiss. You happened to skip a few steps, and those steps were the same ones that most people have tried to skip. Woo her. Treat her like a lady. Show her your affection goes deeper than her appearance because that's what no one has ever taken the time to do."

"How do you know all this?"

She smiled softly at him. "I feel foolish for forgetting, but I remember my mother went through similar issues. No one thought she was good enough for my father and judged him for marrying her years after the fact. Rumors of her being a gold digger, trapping him, the list went on and on. I used to get in fights all during school about it."

"When did it stop?" Bart asked curiously. He'd never heard any stories about Grandma Seever being ostracized or looked down on. Then again, that probably wasn't the kind of story a grandmother would tell her grandchildren.

"Right about when we moved out here. Turns out changing your environment could do an awful lot of good. Because the folks here didn't know her as she looked when she was younger, they only saw a beautiful, yet respectable housewife."

"That's just not right."

"No, it's not. And I'm more than a bit embarrassed that it may have been in the back of my mind." She heaved a large sigh. "I guess it's just so easy to listen to gossip and want to believe you're better than somebody else, even if it's baseless."

Bart leaned over and kissed her cheek. "She already accepted your apology, Ma. Thank you for telling me this."

"Of course. You're my boy, and I think you could do right by her, if you get your head on straight and treat her like a woman should be treated."

"I'd like nothing more, Ma."

"Good. Then I suppose you better cook up a plan and get to it. The longer she thinks you're just like everyone else, the more the idea will stick."

"Right. That makes sense." Bart stood, ready to take action, only to realize that he didn't know exactly *where* to take action.

"Uh…"

"She's out at the edge of the farthest pen, mending fences with Benji."

He shot her a dazzling smile. "Thanks, Ma."

There probably weren't words to explain how monumentally stupid he had been, but all Bart could hope was that Missy had it in her to forgive him.

Again.

...maybe he should go get some flowers first.

20

───────

Bart

By the time Bart managed to get a decent bouquet and a gift certificate to an online pet shop, it was nearing late afternoon. He knew he had to hurry if he wanted to catch Missy.

And boy did he want—no, *need*—to catch Missy. There were so many words in his head, so many emotions in his heart. He knew that he had messed up, but he wanted to set this right. If only she could see how hard he was kicking himself, maybe then she would have some mercy.

Of course, since Missy was like no other woman, he should have approached her like no other woman. He should have known that. And maybe if he wasn't, well, who he was, he *would* have known that.

Too late to go back and try to change it. The only thing he

could do now was make it better. Prove that he wasn't like all those other people who might have misjudged her.

Instead of parking his car and trying to pace across their large property, he took one of the lesser used paths, his truck bouncing along as he probably went faster than he should have. But there was no time for caution, no time to take it easy.

In truth, waiting another day was impossible. The thought that Missy had spent even one night with the idea in her head that he didn't care about her, that he saw her as a loose woman that he could mess around with and forget, made his blood boil and his heart hurt. She didn't deserve that. No, she deserved the *most,* and if she gave him a chance, he'd like to think he could give that to her.

Or at least try. And if he failed, if he ruined it like he ruined everything else, if he ended up more broken than he was before, at least he could say that he had tried.

And it all would have been worth it.

He spotted her and Benji just on the horizon. He was standing in the truck bed, filling his canteen from the large water cooler he kept in the back, while Missy was adamantly digging. He could see from each over-exaggerated jab of her shovel into the ground that she was angry, and it made him wince a bit.

He supposed if she hit him over the head with a shovel, it'd probably be fair play.

Slowly, he pulled up. The last thing he wanted was for one of his wheels to kick a rock up and bean either his brother or Missy. Killing the engine, he stepped out of his truck and gathered his thoughts.

"Whoa, hey, Bart. You're not supposed to be here," Benji said with a start, jumping down to the ground.

Yup. So everyone definitely knew that something went down between him and Missy. He just hoped that all of them framed him as the bad guy and none of them judged her.

"I know. I'll be quick."

"But, I think maybe—"

"It's fine," Missy said, throwing her shovel to the side. "I'm used to guys not taking no for an answer."

She faced him, her hands on her hips, and he could see the pain across her features. It was just awful. He did that to her.

"Missy, it's not like that."

"Isn't it?" she asked, probably a lot more softly than she intended.

He hoped that boded well for him, and he stepped forward, remembering to grab the flowers from the car.

"Really? You think flowers are going to buy you out of this?"

"No," he said, as honestly as he could. "But I was hoping that they would buy me enough time to apologize to you."

That seemed to surprise her, and those little teeth of hers came to worry at her full lip. "Apologize?"

He nodded and took a cautious step forward. They were still a good way apart, but at least he didn't feel like they were in separate rooms now.

"Uh, Miss Dominic, Bart, I wouldn't be lyin' if I said I didn't know what's the thing I'm supposed to do in this situation," Benji said, looking between the two of them.

"It's fine," Missy said. "We can talk. But I'm only giving you five minutes, then I need to head home to feed the little ones."

"Right, of course." He sent a pointed look to Benji, who looked between the two of them once more in confusion before shrugging and getting into his own truck. To his credit, he only pulled about fifteen or so feet away. Enough not to be right on top of the conversation, but close enough if he was needed. Bart appreciated that about his middle brother. Always looking out for others.

Kind of like Missy.

Once he was gone, Bart stepped forward to hand her the flowers. She took them gingerly, far more sweetly than the guarded expression on her face prepared him for, and then smelled them deeply.

"Talk."

"First of all. I'm sorry."

Her eyebrows went up again, and he was reminded of that time he had stood at the foot of her apartment building's stars, looking up at her while she was bathed in sunlight, looking like a renaissance painting made flesh. She'd looked surprised then too, and he wondered just how little she heard those two simple words.

"For what?"

It was clear that she wasn't confused that he was apologizing, but rather that she wanted to hear *what* he was sorry for. She wanted to be sure that he was aware of what he had done wrong and why it wasn't appropriate.

Or at least that was the impression he had. He may have lost a lot of his knack for reading people, but some things were still easy to pick up.

"I'm sorry for rushing things. I'm sorry for kissing you without asking. I'm sorry for assuming that you would be all right with it. I'm sorry that I put what I was feeling ahead of what you were feeling when you've been nothing short of hyper-considerate of my needs." The words grew easier to say as he went along. "I'm sorry that I vaulted over your boundaries without even asking what your boundaries were. I'm sorry I treated you like all the jerks in your life have treated you.

"I promise you, I do not want to be a jerk. In fact, I'd like to be the farthest thing from that, and I can't help but feel like being close to you makes me less of one. And I know that's not your responsibility. You don't owe me therapy, or anything like that. But I'd really, truly hate myself if I ever let you walk away from this ranch not knowing how much I enjoy your company, your talks, and everything else about you."

She didn't say anything for a long while, and he stood there in absolute agony. Part of his mind was taking in how her skin was glistening from a hard day's work, and how her perfect lips were parted as she tried to catch her breath from the strenuous work. Of course, he quickly told that part of his mind to shut up because that wasn't the important matter right now.

"Huh. That was some apology."

"I know it's really not enough to do the situation justice, but I don't think you'd like to stand here and listen to an hour-long soliloquy on my transgressions."

She let out the tiniest smile at that, burying her face in the flowers once more and inhaling. "I dunno, I think I might have a spare night this evening if you want to put on a performance."

"Oh, that's convenient then, because I was hoping to ask you to dinner."

"Wait, what?" She stared at him, face out of the flowers, and looked like that was ten times more shocking than his apology. "You want to go to *dinner*, with me? As in out? Where people could see us?"

"Yes. That's the general idea of how dates work. But if you don't want to, please, please know that it's all right to say no. I don't want you—"

"But I'm not the type of girl who gets asked to dinner."

He stopped short at that, his turn to look at her. "Pardon?"

"You know. I'm the 'drinks at my place' kind of girl. Or 'take a ride through the country' kind of girl. I'm even a 'watch a movie and see what happens' kind of girl. No one asks me to dinner."

Bart's mind tried to churn around that idea. In his defense, he'd had quite a strange couple of days with a whole lot more interaction than he was used to.

"Missy." He tried to keep his tone level, but it was quite difficult given the task. "Are you telling me that you've never been asked to dinner?"

She paused, as if she was *really* thinking hard about it. "Not that I can ever remember, no. I think the last 'date' I was asked on was to the movies by one of the other assistants at the vet clinic, but he kept trying to make out with me, so I left after the opening previews."

Once again that burning feeling filled his chest. The world just didn't make sense.

"Well, I don't know why the rest of this town has been so insane, but Miss Dominic, if you'd be so kind, I'd love to take you to a nice Bistro in the city where we can have a tasty meal. And when we're done, I'd like to drop you off at home, see you to your door, then come right back home where I'm sure my Ma will have a dozen and one questions."

"You say that now, but everyone always tries to pull somethin' at the last min—"

He took one more step forward, affixing her with the most serious look he could muster.

"Missy. Please believe me in that I want to do right by you. You deserve a real, honest-to-God date, and I'd be honored if you gave me another chance."

She eyed him curiously, like she was trying to puzzle something together. Bart felt like he was being plenty clear, but it was hard to say. He'd already bungled so much.

"Why'd you wanna do that?"

"Because you *deserve* that, Missy! That's what I'm trying to say. I'm not gonna stand here and lie by saying I hated the kiss, but I sure did hate how it made you feel. I'd like to make that up to you."

"Even if there's nothing in it for you?" she questioned dubiously.

Geez, it was breaking his heart how she was having such a hard time understanding the concept. What kind of people had she known all her life?

"Missy, that's what I'm trying to say. Your company, and by that, I mean *only* your company and nothing physical, is valuable to me. And to a whole lot of people if they'd just—"

"I have this Friday off."

He blinked, staring at her once more. "Come again?"

"I'm off Fridays and Sundays for now, then Tuesdays, Fridays, and Sundays once winter hits. If you wanna take me to some fancy dinner, Friday night will do."

"All right then," he said with a smile. "I can do that."

"Good. Now I need to finish up this last post before I go. I'll see you then, Bart."

"I'll see you."

He recognized a dismissal when he heard one and went back to his car. But even as he hauled himself up into the truck, he was practically floating on air.

She said yes!

Now he just had to make sure that he didn't mess this date

up too. He had a feeling that if it ever came down to three strikes, he would be out.

21

Missy

Missy finished swiping the lipstick along her lower lip then looked in the mirror. Her nerves were in her stomach, sure that she would look like some sort of overly done up clown, but instead, she saw a sultry woman staring back, all cat-eyeliner and a pouty mouth.

No. That wouldn't do at all either.

Sighing, she wiped it off and reached for her only other lipstick. While she liked the idea that makeup was basically playing with paints on her own face, she didn't like how expensive it was. Heap on top of that that she would only buy cruelty-free products that didn't test on animals, meant she didn't really have a lot of options in her small town and had to rely on the internet.

Buying new makeup on the internet was only slightly less

daunting than buying new shoes on the internet. There was no way to test either of them out first.

Which was largely why she only had two tubes of lipstick. Va-Va-Va-Voom red and Tea and Cookies Pink.

Not that she usually wore makeup out of the house anyway. It encouraged exactly the kind of attention she didn't want. She didn't even know what had possessed her to buy the most-certainly expired red three years ago.

Holding her mouth still, she swiped the much more muted pink across her clean lips. When she finished, she looked up in the mirror to see a slightly less vixen version of Missy staring back at her.

...maybe she should just go without makeup entirely.

No!

This was her first date. A real, honest-to-God date, and she was going to act like a normal person. Besides, Bart said they were going to the city where she wouldn't stick out like a sore thumb. Where people wouldn't see her and know that she was the daughter of the town drunk who had filled out much too early in life.

Missy nodded to herself and went on to tackle the next problem: getting dressed.

As her fingers picked through her meager closet, she couldn't help but think back to that moment just a couple days ago. Bart sweeping up in his truck, looking all classically handsome and muscled and remorseful. She had been all set to dismiss him—it took more than a pretty face to make her crumble—but then he'd been handing her flowers and saying he was sorry. And goodness gracious, looking so sincere that she just about melted right there on the spot.

Was she weak?

Yeah, probably.

But still, a *date*! A real, no-sex-expected, gentleman and lady, *date!*

He could be lying to her. It could be some sort of elaborate trick to get her alone on a country road, but she severely doubted that.

Not with the look he had given her. So earnest. So...*desperate* for her to understand that he'd never want to hurt her.

And if that wasn't such a Bart thing. Strong as a mountain, able to overpower almost everyone she knew, but wanting to be so much more than brute force.

"All right, concentrate Missy. The blue dress or the pantsuit?"

She held up the two outfits she had pulled from her closet, the only ones that seemed close to what a woman should wear on her first date. The blue dress was from online, some site from China that was having a sale. She barely fit into their largest size, but she did. Truthfully, she had wanted it in red, with its fitted top and flaring waist reminding her of the pin-up girls of the forties, but she knew that red was definitely a color she could not wear out in public. It'd be like a literal scarlet letter, except it would be her whole darn dress.

So, she had sprung for blue, which was on her favorite color spectrum. It was cute on her, even if she'd only worn it twice since she bought it.

And the pantsuit had been her almost-graduation present to herself. At first, she just needed a nice outfit for her father's funeral and for the actual graduation ceremony at the end of the school year. But then it'd also turned into her interview outfit as well. It was the outfit she'd worn when she got her job at the veterinarian clinic.

She remembered that day vividly, and as she closed her eyes, she could see slightly-younger Missy wringing her hands with worry. If she stopped to think about it, Missy was pretty sure that she was even more nervous now than she had been back then.

"Breathe," she reminded herself. "You've sat with this guy for hours in the middle of nowhere. You know him. There's no need to be dramatic."

But she couldn't *help* it. Because when she thought of Bart, her mind couldn't help but go back to that *kiss*.

Sure, it had scared the crap out of her. And yeah, it had shattered that delicate layer of trust she had and made her think that he was going to try to use her just like everyone else. She had been so prepared to cut him off to protect herself forever that she hadn't considered the possibility that maybe, just maybe, he was as confused as she was.

After all, it wasn't like the guy didn't have tons on his plate. He was coming down from at least six years in the military, four of them overseas. He couldn't tell her what he did in the military, because he could still only vaguely speak about it. He was a man in recovery from a grievous wound deep inside him.

Certainly, she could afford him a little forgiveness for being so desperate for a little bit of comfort? Of course, she knew she didn't owe *anyone* forgiveness, but when he came to her, full of apologies and assurances that she was so much more than her body, that he cared about *her*, the real her, she wanted to let it go. To try to lower her defenses a little and trust a man who'd been nothing but kind to her—when he was conscious, that was.

So, with all the icky parts forgiven, that only left the nice parts.

And boy were there a lot of nice parts to that kiss.

Did she want another one?

Or did she not want another one?

Enough inner turmoil, she needed to get finished dressing before Bart showed up. And, according to her phone, that was going to be within the next half hour.

The dress. The dress was the winner. It wasn't often that Missy got to be as feminine and fancy as she wanted to, so she was going to do that for the date. She already was pushing herself anyway, why not try to wiggle a bit farther.

She sped through the rest of getting ready, finishing with a pair of stockings and wedges she had bought second hand, and then she was done. With only about twenty more looks into the mirror, she sat down to wait.

Turns out she didn't need to rush at all, and that resulted in her sitting there for ten very anxious minutes until finally, her phone buzzed right on the dot.

I'm here

Oh geez. He was there. In his truck. Waiting to take her to dinner in the city to some sort of fancy place that she was sure she would never be able to afford on her own.

Crap, was this a mistake? Was she even stupider than she had thought earlier this week?

The questions started to buck up again, and Missy hated it. By nature, she was not a shy or insecure person—or at least she liked to think so. Shoving all of those wild thoughts down, she checked her reflection one more time before heading out.

Shoulders broad, spine straight, chin level, she held herself with all the assuredness she had in her body. She could see Bart waiting just outside the door, dressed in a crisp looking blue button-down shirt and dark pants.

Oh. Goodness.

She didn't think it was possible, but he looked even more handsome than he had previously. Missy was pretty sure that was scientifically impossible, yet there she was, staring at him with her mouth slightly open.

"Okay, get yourself together," she murmured to herself before pasting a smile on her face and heading down the rest of the stairs.

Bart offered her an arm and she took it, her heart beating about a million miles an hour as he walked her to the truck, opened the door and then assisted her into the seat. Was this really it? Was it so easy?

It seemed to be as he went around the car and got into the driver's side. He sent her a warm but a bit nervous grin, then they were off.

"I hope you like the restaurant," Bart said after a few moments of quiet driving. "I haven't gone before, but Ben swears by it."

"Oh, does Ben go to the city a lot?"

He shook his head. "Not a lot, I would say. But he's the one who will often meet with new investors, and more often than not, they end up going to dinner."

"Huh, is that bribery or something?" she teased.

"Apparently, that's business."

"Does that mean we're a couple of business people?"

"I'm not sure that's the type of label we want to put on our date."

Oh. Right. Her cheeks colored as she realized the implication of what she had said. "Okay, maybe none of that then."

He chuckled, and that seemed to break the tension between them, then they were back to their usual talking selves.

Granted, did they have a usual? When she thought about it, she actually hadn't known Bart for that long. Which was bizarre considering that she felt like she knew him so well.

Oh well, that was something to ponder when all of her brainpower didn't have to go into making sure she didn't make a mess of the first real date in her entire life.

Wow, no pressure.

Thankfully, they arrived without her going into a blind panic or sticking her foot all the way into her mouth, leaving her entirely free to gape at the beautiful place.

It wasn't so dripping with money and fanciness that she was uncomfortable, but boy was it nice. There was the perfect amount of lighting, and a pleasant sort of rustic feel that probably cost more money than she would ever see in her lifetime.

He whisked her in, her arm once more wrapped through his, and a host in very crisp, white, button-down shirt and black slacks walked them over to a table. After that, their waitress arrived in an equally pressed and pristine outfit. Missy had no idea how they managed it. Even cooking ramen usually left her with at least a spot or two on her shirt.

"So, do you have any recommendations?" Missy asked nervously, a bit intimidated by the thick menu in front of her. Was that leather? It seemed like leather. Wow. This certainly wasn't the town diner.

"I was thinking of just getting the all-American burger."

Missy couldn't stop her snort.

"What?" he asked, looking up at her ruefully.

"Nothing. It's just..." She paused to try to take a breath and center herself. "The all-American burger? Really? You don't think that might be a bit on the nose, Mr. Apple Pie and Patriotism?"

"Mr. Apple—*Really?*"

She snickered, and the nervous feeling from her unfamiliar

surroundings settled a bit more. "I mean, come on, you gotta know that you've got the whole iconic thing going for you."

"What, you mean mental illness and a relatively loose understanding of geography?"

She rolled her eyes. She didn't mind self-deprecation, but usually, she preferred it when it was in jest, and she was pretty sure that Bart believed the negativity he was uttering.

"No. I mean chiseled jaw, rippling muscles, eyes that are *way* too intense to be legal, knows how to work a gun, dedication to the country, *oh,* and literally lives on a massive ranch. You're like, American icon personified."

He rolled his eyes at that, but she noticed the light coloring to his cheeks. Good. In her opinion, a lot of really nice men weren't given compliments as much as they should be. Everyone liked to hear that they looked nice every once in a while.

"American icon?" He shook his head.

"It's a great compliment. You're the personification of everything that our country thinks is great."

He outright snorted at that. It seemed he was picking up on her habits, and she couldn't bring herself to feel sorry about it.

"I dunno, if anyone here is classic Americana, it's you."

She scrunched up her nose, giving him a dubious look. "What? *How*?"

Now it was his turn to smile. "I know you've seen all those World War Two posters with the pin-ups and homemakers that were specifically typed to inspire men and stop them from spinning off into a morale-less void."

"Well yeah, but—"

He gestured up and down to her seated body. "There. You. Classic Americana."

Another snort. If anyone was listening nearby, they probably were quite concerned with the quality of the conversation going on.

"I am not classic Americana."

"Really? How beautiful you are in that classic dress would indicate otherwise."

She rolled her eyes, but she felt her cheeks coloring too. "I'm pretty sure it takes more than the right dress to be a pin-up."

He chuckled again, and she found herself wanting him to make that sound more and more. It was a nice sound. A safe sound. And if she didn't think too hard about why she liked it so much, then maybe her heart would calm down.

"Yeah, but I'm pretty sure you've got it all."

"Do I?" She braced herself, waiting for comments on her figure. She knew that was where the conversation had to go, and she knew that she was goading him toward saying something that she wouldn't like. Why? She didn't know. Maybe she just wanted to sabotage things early so that her heart wouldn't be broken when it inevitably went down in flames.

"Yeah. I mean, you've got the hair, the smile, and that look in your eyes that's kinda daring someone to try to talk to you."

Oh. That hadn't been what she was expecting. "Are you saying that I'm hard to talk to?"

"Only you would take it that way," He leaned forward a bit, as if they were speaking conspiratorially. And she liked it. "Beautiful, intelligent women are always hard to talk to. They're intimidating."

Missy preened at that. Which was probably weird, but she liked the thought that someone might be scared to talk to her because of her sharp tongue. It was like a gold star. "Huh, for being intimidated, you certainly seem to have an easy time talking to me."

"Oh, so you admit that you think you're beautiful and intelligent?" he said taunting, wiggling his eyebrows at her.

Goodness, she didn't think they'd ever been so relaxed around each other, and it was doing a whole lot for her.

She flicked a bit of water at him and laughed. "Of course. Has there ever been a doubt of that?"

"Huh, and there's that cockiness from all those posters too. Proof that of the two of us, you are definitely the epitome of Americana."

Missy shook her head, having way too much fun. "This is a really bizarre conversation."

"Yeah... yeah, it is. But I'm glad you're here to have it."

And her whole face flushed all at once. What was happening? She was not normally this... *reactive* to people. But interacting with Bart made her feel like her entire body was all one raw nerve, sensitive and tense. In the best way possible.

Their waitress brought their drinks after that and then took their order. Not too much later, they were stuffing their faces while regaling each other with stories of old. She told him about high school, and how she rescued her first animal when she was ten. She touched on pretty much anything that wasn't too depressing. Or at least depressing in her opinion, but sometimes Bart's expression changed to mildly upset or angry, which told her maybe her scale of judging things wasn't the most accurate.

He told her about the mischief he got into when he was younger, as well as a ton of stories about his brothers. The only thing he completely avoided was any military stories beyond basic training. She didn't mind, and she certainly didn't ask, but she hoped that one day he would be able to think about those memories without pain.

The conversation went on long after the meal ended, and the

minutes quickly turned to hours. Before Missy knew it, the waitress was coming by to say they were just fifteen minutes away from closing.

"Wow, how did that happen?" she asked, standing and looking around feeling guilty.

"Good conversation," Bart answered matter-of-factly, pulling two hundreds from his wallet and placing them on the table. "Hopefully that will make up for camping so long."

Missy gave him another look over. "You're rich. How do you know what camping is?" Sure, it was a pretty common phrase in her world, but in her experience rich people live in their own kind of reality where they didn't think about how them hogging a table might affect a tip-reliant waitress.

He laughed quietly. "Ma wasn't always married to Pa. She waited tables when she was younger, so she drilled all that proper dining-out etiquette into us since we were old enough to understand what money actually was."

"Huh."

"Huh?" he repeated, coming around the table to give her his arm again. "What does that mean?"

"You're full of surprises, aren't you?"

The top of his killer cheekbones colored ever so slightly again. "Maybe. I'm trying to keep them to the good surprises kind of thing."

Without thinking, she pulled him closer so that their sides were almost flush. Huh. That was bold of her. "You're definitely on the good side so far."

"Good."

They headed out toward his truck again, and Missy was tempted to rest her head on his shoulder. But she wasn't exactly sure if that would feel great considering that they were in motion, and before she could decide one way or another, a booming voice called out from behind them.

"Ay, Miller! Is that you?"

They both turned, and she saw another strapping man with a pretty woman walking with him. He was shorter than Bart, but much broader, with so many muscles on his shoulder that he had that kind of froggy-looking, overly built aesthetic to him.

"Jacob?" Bart asked, looking to the man with the most shocked expression that Missy had ever seen him wear.

"Yeah man, it's me! Oh man, I haven't seen you in forever. How have you been?"

Before Missy could really figure out if this chance encounter was a good or a bad thing, the man was crossing the space to them quickly. Like an old friend, he hugged Bart tightly, his big hands clapping him twice on the back. Hard, in a brothers-in-arms kind of way.

Missy saw Bart stiffen, and she figured out that no, it wasn't a good thing, real fast.

The man—Jacob—pulled back, but his grip was still strong on Bart's arms. "I'm sorry we lost touch, but man, it's good to see you here!" He turned and looked to the woman next to him. "I wouldn't be alive if it weren't for this guy. We were driving along one night when suddenly it was a whole firefight. He practically threw me under cover because I was so green that I froze on the spot. Would have gotten swiss-cheesed for sure."

"I'm so sorry," Missy cut in, alighting her hands on one of his and tugging on it. "But I think Bart would rather not talk about his time overseas right now. And he doesn't like being surprised by touch."

"He doesn't... what?" To the man's credit, he did back away. "Bart, who's this? What's she talking about?"

"I..." Bart gasped, squeezing his eyes shut. She knew that look. It was the same expression he wore when he broke out of the haze that had made him attack her. But given the situation, she was pretty sure that he was sliding into that place instead of freeing himself from it. "This isn't—"

The man crowded Missy again, trying to reach his friend, to comfort him. Missy understood the sentiment, but it wasn't the place or time.

"Hey, buddy, you all right?"

But Missy knocked his hand away before he could touch. She could feel the tension from Bart behind her, drawn so tight that she was afraid one more thing would have him shattering in dozens of little pieces.

"*Please,*" she murmured. "He's still adjusting."

"Adjusting?" Finally, the man backed off, but he seemed plenty hurt.

Missy wasn't sure if it was because he was perceiving this as some sort of rejection, or if it was because he was looking at what very well could have happened to him.

Jacob gave one last attempt. "All right, buddy. Maybe we can talk later?"

Bart didn't say anything, but Missy didn't want this Jacob to never be able to connect with him. What to say and still protect his privacy?

"There are a lot of group meetings at the VA support center in this city," she said. "Maybe sometime you guys will run into each other there."

"Support center? All right. You be safe, okay? I miss ya, buddy. I'd like to catch up sometime."

"I'm sure he'd like that too. But we should really get home."

"Right. Goodnight, Miss..."

"Dominic," she answered firmly. "It was nice to meet you, Jacob."

"Yeah, I'm not so sure about that."

Jacob and his lady skirted around them, heading off in the other direction. With the distraction gone, Missy turned to Bart to see that his face was pale, and his eyes were scuttling back and forth, like he was trying to figure out what was real and what wasn't.

"Bart," she asked quietly. "Where are you right now?"

He took a ragged breath, and it cut her right down to the bone. "I don't know."

"Okay. That's all right. You're somewhere safe. Whatever you're seeing, wherever you think you are, I promise you're safe."

"I..." How was it possible for someone to look like he was in so much pain? "I can hear it. All of it."

She didn't need to ask him what "it" was. Taking a deep breath to steady herself, she forced herself to only exude calm and comfort. It wasn't easy.

"Bart, honey, can you hear me?"

He nodded, swallowing several times. He looked so scared. She didn't want him to have that fear inside of him anymore.

"Okay, I'm going to touch you now. I'm going to take your keys from your pocket. Is that all right?"

He didn't answer, but it seemed like he still heard her. She was acutely reminded of what happened the last time she had tried to initiate contact when he was in a fugue, but she pushed that aside. Bart deserved her trust.

Her hand shook as she reached out, but this time there was no lash, no recoil as her fingers gently traced the edge of his pocket. It only took a little bit of wiggling before her digits found a keyring, and then she was pulling them into her grasp.

"Come on," she said, her hand gently alighting on his elbow. "Let's just go to the truck."

"No good. The trucks gone."

"What, no it's not, it's just—"

He shook his head vehemently. "It was a mine. Blew the back half off."

Oh. Right. Something entirely different was happening for him. She didn't want to know what memory he was seeing. She just wanted him out of it.

"Sorry, I didn't realize," she murmured. "What transport do we have, Bart? What's safe to take?"

"The end of the caravan. We can provide cover while we fall back."

"All right, let's do that then. We're falling back."

She walked him slowly, carefully, until they reached the parking garage. Bart didn't say much, his body stiff and jerky like he was a robot, and she felt like she was a pile of jelly by the time they reached the side of the truck.

She opened the passenger side and pushed him in, careful as she buckled him in. "We're gonna get you home now, okay?"

"What about the others?" he asked. "We have to check for them. I don't want anyone caught under the wheels. We don't leave people behind."

Wow. That was a whole lot to unpack there. But she didn't have time to. She needed to take care of the man in front of her.

"You got them all," Missy said, gently cupping his face. "I promise, you saved all of them. No one is left behind."

"No one?"

"No one."

He nodded, his eyes scanning the garage, but she knew he didn't really see it. "Okay. Let's go."

"Yeah, let's do that."

She closed the door and rushed around the car, her fingers shaking as she turned the key in the ignition. Gripping the gearshift, she headed for the long drive home.

To his credit, Bart seemed way more lucid than he had been the first two times she had met him. Back then he had been shaking, and non-verbal, his eyes empty of anything other than pain and fear. Now he could kinda talk, and he seemed to react okay to stimuli, such as red lights or another driver cutting them off.

That was good, right?

Missy didn't know, and she wished she had done even more research on PTSD. Bart's didn't exactly express itself as her father's had.

"Where are you taking me?" Bart asked, suddenly sitting up and nearly giving Missy a heart attack only fifteen minutes into their drive.

"Just home, Bart. It's okay. You're safe."

"Home? No. This is the wrong way." His tone grew sharp and angry. Not like her Bart. Oh geez, she remembered reading about the suspicion and aggression that sometimes set in. "Take me to the camp."

"We're going to the camp," she tried to say assuredly.

"No! This is wrong. It's all wrong." His hand reached over to grip the wheel. Missy steeled both of her arms, holding on for dear life as he tried to yank.

"Bart! Bart, I need you to calm down. We're going the right way, I promise."

He looked at her, his hard pull easing slightly. "I don't understand."

"It's okay. I promise. I'm taking you back to camp." His

fingers lightened a bit again, and Missy scrambled for something to soothe him. Her mind went back to that first night when she hadn't known what to do besides hum the same lullaby that had helped her when she was younger.

Carefully, softly, she started singing, somewhere just above a whisper.

His eyes widened ever so slightly, and he sat back. "I don't understand," he repeated.

"I know," she said, her heart aching and hammering at the same time. It wasn't a very pleasant sensation. "But don't worry. I've got you."

She went back to humming, and he settled back into his seat, his eyes eventually drifting shut. His body stayed tense, however, so she tried to give him his space.

Occasionally, his hand would reach out, brushing along her arm, or gripping her shirt, but that was as far as it went. It felt like more of a way to ground himself rather than attack her, so she let him do whatever he needed.

After what felt like forever, she was on the long driveway to the house. Skipping the path to the flat expanse she normally parked on, she pulled right over the lawn and up to the porch steps.

She risked a quick beep on the horn, which startled Bart into an upward position, but thankfully that was it. Hurriedly, she hopped out of the driver's side and went around to his door.

Footsteps sounded behind her, and soon she was flanked by more tall bodies.

"What happened?" the eldest, Ben, asked.

"He's having an episode," Missy answered, trying to keep her voice level like it wasn't a big deal. "He ran into one of his old military buddies who accidentally triggered him."

"Triggered him how?" That was Benji, the middle one.

"Couple of hard slaps on the back, a tight hug, hands on his arms, and talking about an old fight."

"Crap," Ben hissed before leaning into the car. "Hey, little bro. It's me. Think you can come out now?"

Bart looked to him blearily, clearly quite confused. "Ben, how are you here?"

"It's not a big deal. How about we go in and put you to bed?"

"Bed?" he repeated.

His brothers reached out cautiously, helping the man to his feet. Now that the worst of it had passed, it seemed that he was about to pass out, all the strength flushed from him. Missy watched, chewing on her lips, as they wrangled him up the porch and into the house.

She stood there, truck still running behind her when she felt soft hands gently pull at her own fingers. Blinking, she realized that Mrs. Miller had walked up to her, all soft smiles in her nightgown.

"Hello dear, why don't you come in?"

Wait. *In?* As in, inside the house? Last time that had happened, it hadn't exactly ended well for her.

"Oh no, that's fine. I'll just..." she trailed off, her eyes still on Bart as he rounded a corner and left her vision.

"Please. I think he'd want you here."

"Okay." She willed her legs into motion and allowed herself to be pulled along by the matriarch. But as she was led into the house, her worry about herself sort of faded into the background, and her whole mind was centered on one furtive concern.

She just wanted him to be okay.

22

____

Bart

Consciousness smacked into Bart like he had done something to insult its honor. His heart jumped into his throat, his teeth clamped shut, and his breath hitched before suddenly he was sitting up, covered in sweat.

What had happened? The last thing he remembered, he was having the best date he could have ever hoped for with Missy. But nothing about that memory lead to him being in bed, still dressed in his clothes that were rumpled and a bit damp.

For a moment an idea flashed across his mind, and he looked beside himself to see if Missy was there, wondering if somehow, he hadn't been the gentleman he had set out to be. He was both relieved and disappointed to see that she wasn't there.

"Hey, you want a glass of water?"

Stiffly, Bart turned his head to see his brother, Ben, sitting in a chair beside the bed, a pitcher and couple of glasses on the nightstand next to him.

"Ugh. Yes," he managed to rasp. His mouth felt like he had tried to swallow a whole stick of chalk.

His brother smiled weakly and went about handing him a glass. Bart gulped it down, taking inventory of the situation as he did.

It was daytime now, but still early judging by where the sun was outside his window. Only his brother was present, but he could hear the everyday chatter downstairs.

Setting his glass down, Bart leaned back against his head-board. "What happened?" He tried not to guess, tried not to let his mind cook up a million and one awful ideas about how he ended up in his bed with his clothes still on.

"You had an episode."

"Ah." Bart held out the glass for his brother to refill then gulped that down too. "Is this the part where you tell me that I did that *after* arriving home, having successfully dropped Missy off at her apartment?"

Ben's lips went thin, and he shook his head. "Sorry. She's actually the one who brought you here. Drove all the way from the city."

"I see."

He knew it was a stilted response, but what was he supposed to say? She'd given him a third chance, and he had blown that too by literally checking right out of reality.

He should have known better. He didn't deserve a woman like her anyway, all fire and compassion and beauty. He was a fool to think that he even had a chance, that he somehow was enough to take her on those dates she so deserved.

"Hey, are you all right?" Ben asked cautiously, his hand gently reaching out for Bart's shoulders.

"Yeah. It's nothing I didn't expect."

"Bart—" Ben said reproachfully.

"It's fine. Really. What other way could it have worked out?"

But he wished it had. She was the first woman he had really *seen* since he came back. She was something special, a one of a kind soul that he didn't think he'd ever meet again.

And he had ruined it.

He certainly had a knack for that, didn't he?

"Look," Ben said, cutting through his spiraling mood. "Before you delve off that cliff in your mind, how about we eat some breakfast. I'm sure you could use some food in you."

"Yeah, sure. Moping on a full stomach is better for me anyway, I'm sure."

"That's the spirit!"

Bart pushed himself out of bed and followed his brother downstairs. He paused at his door, however, looking down at himself.

"Hey. You go on ahead, okay. I'm gonna change."

"Sounds like a plan."

Maybe it wasn't the best time to be alone, but Bart appreciated a few more minutes to gather himself. He felt a sort of despondent apathy in him, but that was about it. He supposed the rest of the feelings of worthlessness —with a side of derision —would come when he was a bit more awake and his failure really sunk in.

He picked a simple T-shirt and some jeans, ran a comb through his hair and then headed down. While food couldn't really solve his problem, he didn't see how several helpings of bacon and sausage would hurt.

It was right when he got to the bottom of the stairs that he stopped short, his gaze caught a familiar smile that never failed to make his heart rate speed up.

Missy was sitting at the table with his brothers, chuckling at something that he hadn't heard. His mind scrambled to figure out what the heck was going on.

She was still in that beautiful dress from last night, her hair mussed from sleep and her eyes still a bit heavy-lidded. Her eyeliner was a little smeared, but to him, she was quite the heavenly sight.

"Missy, what are you doing here?" he heard himself ask far too breathlessly for a grown man.

She looked up at him and beamed so brightly that he was sure that the sun had to be jealous. "Glad to see you're awake. You better sit down before I eat all the biscuits."

He sat down at the table across from her, his eyes never leaving her face. She blushed and returned to the food and conversation that had been going on before he had arrived. Bart didn't contribute, just watching and trying to figure out if this was real life or a very convincing dream.

Eventually, however, even his Ma and Pa were at the table, and everyone was digging in like absolutely nothing was wrong.

Something wasn't making sense, and for once he was pretty sure that it wasn't him.

"Ben, I hope you don't mind giving me an hour or two to go to my place and get changed into something a bit more work appropriate for the rest of the day?" That was Missy, of course, looking up from her plate that was still fairly full of food.

"Oh no, that's not appropriate at all!" Ma interjected. For a moment Bart felt himself prickle—what, did she want Missy to work in heels and a dress? But then she continued, "You did much for our family yesterday. Take the day off. Paid of course." Her eyes flicked from Bart to her. "Besides, I feel there might be some things you need to talk about."

That was putting it lightly.

"Thank you," Missy said, her cheeks coloring slightly. "I'd like that."

"Of course, dear. You're basically family now, so you might as well enjoy it."

At that, Missy looked right down at her plate and didn't glance up until the end of the meal.

Which, in Bart's opinion, couldn't happen fast enough. He had been itching to talk to her since his mind got over the shock that she was in front of him and didn't seem to be recoiling in horror.

Going around the table as his brothers helped clear the dishes, Bart almost reached out for her arm but stopped at the last moment.

"May I walk you out?" he asked, his voice sounding strange even to him.

She nodded, looping her arm through his in an echo of their date the previous night. Except then their date hadn't been colored by him flying off the handle and having another episode right in front of her.

It was an incredibly low bar to be grateful that he hadn't strangled her again, wasn't it?

Of course, it didn't take long for them to reach the porch and then get to his truck, which was not parked in its usual spot. Curious. But he could ask questions about it later.

"Is it ok if I give you a ride home?" he asked, almost cringing at his hesitance. Why would she want to be alone with him? He had no idea how he had acted during his episode. He vaguely remembered sliding into the darkness as fire rained down all around him, but he guessed that it probably wasn't anywhere near normal. At all.

But despite all that, she smiled softly at him, her sleepy expression still lingering a bit around her eyes. "Yeah. That'd be nice."

Nice? He could work with that.

"All right. Let me go grab my keys. I'll be right back."

"You don't have to worry about that, your brother left them on the seat."

"He did?" Bart asked, a bit confused.

She nodded. "I drove your truck right up to the porch, you should have seen it. Later, once you were settled and they gave you your medicine, Bradley parked it over here."

"Ah. I see."

How embarrassing. But also, impressive that she knew how to drive a stick. Most people didn't learn that skill nowadays unless they had to.

He walked her to her side and opened the door for her before returning to his side. Hopping in, he started it up and slowly backed out. He wanted to say something to her as they rode along. To come up with some excuse for his blackout, but there really wasn't an excuse for it.

He'd gone to war as one person and came back different. He was still trying to reunite those two jagged halves, and he wasn't quite there yet. Although he was going to continue to go to his therapist, continue attending meetups, there were going to be more episodes in the future. That was just the way it would have to be in his journey toward being healthy and whole.

For the moment, that was his reality, and there was no escaping it.

They rode together in silence, the road stretching before them, taking her away from him and back toward safety.

23

Missy

They drove along in silence, Missy not quite sure what to say.

She was well aware that she had seen Bart in quite a vulnerable state for the second time since they'd known each other, and he probably wasn't the most comfortable with that. When he'd first seen her at the breakfast table, his face had a mix of shock and embarrassment. There was a whole lot to say, but she didn't know quite how to word it.

But since the night previous, she'd come to a solid conclusion, and she wanted to tell him that. It was hard to find a way to bring it up, and since he was being so silent, she didn't want to blurt it out like a random thought.

But time was running out because then he was parking, and after that, he was walking her to her door. His spine was stiff again as her arm wrapped around his, but he didn't flinch away at her contact.

Sweat began to bead at her brow as they grew closer and closer to the door of her building. She needed to get the words out. Just say something, *anything!* As nice as it would be to wimp out, that wouldn't be doing right by him.

Finally, they reached the flat landing before the door, and she took a deep breath. But before she could utter a single phrase, Bart was the one who spoke first.

"Some date, huh?"

Huh, she had expected a little more self-deprecation than that. Or him telling her it wouldn't work between them because of some depressing reason.

"I had fun, actually."

His eyes seemed to widen at that. "You did?"

She nodded, allowing herself to smile softly. "Yeah. Not bad for a first try."

There was that slight smirk that she missed so much. "You know what they say, practice makes perfect."

She let go of his arm and allowed herself to take a step closer to him, crowding him a little. "Are you saying that you'd like to take me on another date?"

The corner of his mouth went up even higher. "Are you saying you *want* me to take you on another date?"

"Of course. Like I said, I had fun, and you really were the perfect gentleman. My only fear is that I might get spoiled."

He sputtered for a moment, clearly confused, and she sensed that this conversation was about to get a whole lot less flirty. That was a shame. She was starting to maybe, finally understand the whole flirting business in general.

"I had an episode!"

"I know. I was there."

"But—I don't..." he squinted his eyes at her like she wasn't making sense. Which, she supposed to him, she wasn't. "How could that be a good date?"

She allowed herself one more tiny half step, and they were almost flush. She could feel his breath on her face again, and it would be so easy to go up on the tip of her toes and make him forget all that pain behind his eyes with a heated kiss.

But that was the easy path, and neither of them needed that.

"It's fine. You were hurting, and you needed help. That's like holding it against someone for having an allergic reaction on a date, or an asthma attack. It was a medical emergency, and I am glad that I was there to help. I've got enough experience with rescues not to be bothered by something like that."

He just breathed for several seconds, and she felt like maybe he was ordering his thoughts. "Is that what I am?" he asked, sounding almost terrified of her answer. "A wounded animal lucky enough to have you swoop in and save me?"

Ah. She could see how he might get that impression. Time to kick that out.

"No," she answered calmly, lifting her arms to wrap around his shoulders. "I've never wanted to kiss one of my animals. At least not how I'd like to kiss you."

His face flushed, no doubt matching hers, and she could feel his broad muscles tensing under her arms. "You want to kiss me again?"

"I do," she answered before slowly pulling away. "But how about after a fully successful date where we can actually try that whole goodnight kiss at the door thing."

The resulting grin on his face nearly blinded her. Goodness, he was handsome. God was not playing fair when he made the Miller boys, that was for sure.

"I think that's a good idea," he said, his hands coming up to rest on his sides. She could feel his thumbs gently stroking the material of her dress, but he managed not to pull her closer. Which was good, because if he did, she didn't think she could resist the urge to crash her lips against his own.

"Where do you want to go? And when?" he asked.

"Well, I'm free this Sunday night. I know things close early, but I make a mean lasagna." She looked up at him, smiling softly. "How do you feel about Italian?"

There was still some part of her, in the very back of her mind, that was worried about trusting him. Trusting anyone. It whispered that she was never meant for romance, and he was going to use her just like everyone else tried to.

But it was easier to drown out that voice now because she'd had a revelation as she'd laid in the Miller's guest room.

And it was that—even though he was obviously attracted to her—he saw her as a person. As Melissa Dominic. He saw her personality. He saw her flaws. He made her laugh, and he made her feel safe. While he appreciated her body, it was nowhere near even the top reason why he wanted her close.

And she felt drawn toward him in a way she had never been drawn to anyone else. He put her at ease in a way no one else could, and she found herself dreaming of a future she never thought possible for herself.

Maybe it was too soon to say something like love. Maybe this was just some sort of meet-cute crush. Missy really had no way of knowing, but for the first time in her life, she was willing to take the chance and find out.

"Italian sounds great," Bart answered, tilting his head down to rest his forehead against hers. And just like she knew he would, he respected her wish not to kiss at that moment. "I'm looking forward to it."

"Me too," she said. "Me too."

EPILOGUE

Bart

"*O*h, just as a reminder, the Christmas Fundraiser is coming up. Dillon told me that you signed up to help with the event?"

"Yeah," Bart said, gazing out the window and only half listening. "Is that an issue?"

His therapist sat back, regarding him with a pleasant smile on his face. "Not at all. I just know that you're not exactly comfortable around large social gatherings. What caused the change of heart?"

"You know exactly what," Bart said, his eyes not leaving the window. Snow was beginning to fall gently outside, but it didn't seem to be too thick or clinging. Hopefully, they had another week or so before it got really bad.

"Ah. Miss Dominic again?"

Bart nodded.

"I see. And how is she?"

"Good," he answered shortly. "Perfect. Beautiful. Crazy for being with me. You know, the usual." He managed to pry his eyes from the window and gave his therapist a wan smile. "She's cooking half of the food for the fundraiser with Ma. I swear, the two of them together are practically unstoppable."

"I can imagine from what you've told me about the two of them." He chuckled for a moment before regarding his notebook.

Bart liked this guy. He was a vet himself, having gotten out maybe seven or so years before Bart did, and used his GI bill to finish his schooling for therapy. Or whatever was the official degree that led to becoming a shrink. He didn't seem out of touch and scholarly like the stereotype but had a calm sort of collectedness to him that Bart wished he had.

"Before we wrap up, can you tell me what the significance of this date is?"

Bart eyed him curiously, quickly going through things in his head. It wasn't a family member's birthday, and certainly not Missy's. He'd bought her a weekend getaway to a spa in the city, along with one of his girl-cousins that she'd made friends with after working together during the winter. It wasn't Christmas yet. He really couldn't think of what was so important.

"Am I missing something, doc?"

"You've been episode free for six months. That's a record for you."

Bart blinked at him for a couple of moments, his mind trying to see if that was accurate. Sure enough, the last time he had an episode was three weeks or so after he and Missy started going steady. He'd gotten close a few times, but he didn't feel that same forlorn despair that let him slip into the dark so easily.

"Huh. So it is."

"I think that's something to celebrate. You've made some miraculous progress in your healing. It's just important to remember that when—and I mean when not if—an episode happens again, to pick yourself up and keep going for a new record."

"Yeah, yeah. I'm aware. I won't get too big for my britches. Besides, I have plenty of other stuff to worry about."

"Indeed, you do. Are you ready for all of that? You're taking some very big steps. Bart. Steps you once told me you thought you'd never be able to take."

"Yeah, guess I was wrong. I'm wrong about a lot of things."

"So are most people." He smiled and stood, setting his notebook on his desk. "I think we're good on not meeting until after the new year. I'm proud of you, Bart. I'm excited to see where your life is taking you."

"You and me both," Bart agreed with a wry grin, standing as well and shaking his hand. "I'll see you next year."

His therapist walked him out of the office where his brother was already waiting with his truck. Bart slid into the passenger seat, his stomach flopping around.

"Is everything in place?" Bart asked.

"Yup. Everyone's heading toward the restaurant. Just waiting for us."

"Then what are you waiting for? Get us to the city."

"Impatient much?" Ben asked, laughing lightly as he put the car into gear.

"What can I say? When Ma calls a lunch for the whole family, you make sure you get there in a reasonable time."

"*Sure*," Ben said, rolling his eyes but smiling nonetheless, and they headed out.

And while he didn't speed *too* badly, Ben put the pedal a little bit to the metal as they rushed toward the city. They were headed toward a very special restaurant, one that his Ma had insisted would be perfect for the day.

They arrived only a bit after everyone else, which was just what he hoped. Crossing over to his seat next to Missy, he sat down with a sigh.

"How was the doctor's?" Missy asked after pressing a gentle kiss to the side of his cheek.

He wanted to answer, but like usual, she took his breath away. Her hair had grown even longer in the little over half-year that they had started dating, and she had the blond tresses piled atop her head like a crown. She was wearing that stylized eyeliner that drove him up the wall in the best way and red lipstick.

Goodness, as if he didn't have a hard enough time looking away from her full lips as it was. It was like she was purposefully attempting to try him, and he absolutely loved it.

"Fine," he answered, catching her chin to turn her face toward his and plant a quick kiss right on those perfect lips of hers.

She pulled away, chuckling slightly. "As verbose as ever, I see."

"Of course."

Rolling her eyes, she returned to whatever conversation she was having with the cousin next to her, leaving Bart to fidget while menus were passed around and orders were decided.

Thankfully, with all of his family and friends and everyone surrounding him, it was easy to get caught up in the comfort and happiness of the crowd, rather than being overwhelmed by the sights and the sounds.

Missy's hand slid into his as they ordered, two waiters taking care of their whole family. They were at a Greek place, which Missy was excited about considering she had an ardent love of baklava, so he went basic with a gyro and lots of tzatziki sauce.

But it wasn't the food on his mind really. Not even hardly.

After the meals arrived, they enjoyed a fun family dinner full of lively conversation.

"How about we all have some dessert?" Ben suggested after most everyone was done eating.

Bart's stomach flipped. "Yeah, dessert sounds good."

The waiters returned, and after some hemming and hawing, everyone started to pick out what they wanted.

Except for Missy. She seemed to be stuck.

"What's the dilemma?" Bart asked, looking over her shoulder to look at the dessert menu. When they had first gone out, he remembered that she would rarely order anything after a meal, stating she didn't want to be greedy. It had taken at least a month to convince her that it was perfectly normal to order a dessert and that he was more than happy to treat her.

In fact, treating her was often one of the things he looked forward to most.

"I dunno. I kinda want the cheesecake, but I kind of want the chocolate orb."

"Chocolate orb?" he asked, trying to sound normal. "What's that?"

"It's this thing where it's like a sphere, and you pour a heated sauce over it, and it melts to reveal a dessert."

Huh. That was pretty lucky. "That sounds nice. You should get that."

"You think so?"

"Yeah, definitely."

"Thanks, babe." She pressed another kiss to his cheek, and it tugged at his heart like it did every other time.

She put in her order, and Bart found each minute ticking by at a snail's pace. It was hard for his palms not to sweat in her grip, and he pulled his hand from her gently. If she thought anything of it, she didn't say, just continued laughing with Chastity and a couple of his cousins.

But of course, his eyes never left her the whole time. He took in everything about her, once more trying to burn every single detail of these moments into his mind for all eternity. The elegant curve of her neck, the strong line of her shoulders, the bright light in her eyes that everyone seemed to fall in love with.

Ma said that Missy had blossomed since they had gotten together, but Bart knew what it really was. Missy had always been an exemplary, enchanting woman, she just trusted so few people that she never really let anyone see the real her.

He could not be more grateful that—for some reason that was still beyond him—she had chosen to show that side of her to him.

To think, it had all started with sleepwalking, and now he was sure he was staring at the love of his life.

The waiters joined them once again, this time with two more workers to help them, and everybody cheered. But Bart couldn't quite get the noise to come out of his throat, and he found himself continuing to stare at the beautiful woman that he could never truly deserve but would spend all of his life trying to.

"What?" she asked, blushing a bit as she caught his stare. She tucked a bit of hair behind her ear as the pink traveled down her face and into her neck. "Do I have something in my teeth?"

"No," he answered as levelly as he could. "You're beautiful."

She was so adorable when she was flustered, and the way she looked down at the table while her blush deepened took away some of his nerves.

The waiters served her last—of course—placing the orb in front of her with a bit of dramatic relish. "And for the lady," he said before pouring the hot chocolate sauce over the beautiful sphere. Of course, everyone fell silent, knowing what was waiting for her, what Bart had been planning since two months into their relationship.

Bit by bit it melted, revealing a truly decadent piece of cake underneath. But Missy didn't seem to see the confection at all, her eyes instead homing in on the small, plastic orb sitting on top of it.

"Is... is that a ring box I see in there?" she whispered, her voice barely audible even from where he was sitting.

"I don't know," he whispered right back. "Why don't you open it and see?"

Her hands were shaking as she reached for it, pulling the orb off the cake and pressing the button in the center to pop it open. Not minding the chocolate on her fingertips, she took out the velvet box and cautiously opened it.

"Oh my, Bart!"

Tears were already springing into her eyes, and Bart gently took the ring from her grip, his other hand pulling one of hers toward him. The ring was a simple band, with one sparkling diamond, and a loving inscription inside. The band was made from platinum because she'd told him how much she hated gold. The inscription was short, but simple, and had been the same words her father had said to her mother on their own wedding day.

"It's perfect," Missy said, her voice cracking.

Bart pushed away from the table and got down on one knee, heart thumping again.

"Melissa Dominic," he said. He saw her breath hitch, and her whole upper body started to shake. He wanted to reach up and comfort her, to tell her that everything was all right, but he had to get the words out before he chickened out.

"You are the most perfect woman I have ever met, and every single day, I learn a little bit more of just how wonderful you are. You are caring, strong, kind-hearted, patient and a precious jewel. I love bringing a smile to your lips and joy to your eyes. I love treating you as you deserve.

"I can't imagine what my life would be like if you hadn't found me on that hill, cold and alone. But then you were there, risking everything for someone you didn't know. Caring like only you would. You were crazy." Everyone laughed at that. "But exactly the kind of crazy I needed.

"When you took my hand, neither of us knew it, but our lives changed forever. You've helped me grow, heal and become a better man. You've shown me there's so much more to look forward to, more possibilities than I could have ever hoped for.

"And if just these six months could be so amazing, then I can't wait to see what the rest of our lives can bring us."

He took a deep breath. This was it. The fateful words.

"Melissa Dominic, will you do me the honor of marrying me?"

"Yes! Yes! Oh, my God, *yes!*" She flung herself forward, her arms going around his shoulders and her lips crashing to his. It was only his upper strength that kept the two of them from pitching backward, so he held her as her lips pressed everything she felt into him.

He returned it with all the passion he had, devouring her like he wanted to, never taking for granted all the feelings of love and desire and safety she caused in him.

Who knows how long they would have kept at it, but eventually someone cleared their throat, prompting Bart to pull away.

"Right. I guess there's one more thing to do."

He took her hand in his own, and with his other, he slid the ring onto the appropriate finger. "For now, and forever," he said, his heart swelling.

"For now, and forever," she repeated, leaning down to kiss him once more.

This time it was soft and slow, tender promises of all the beautiful things they had in store for each other. Bart felt Missy's tears spill a bit onto his own cheeks, but he didn't mind. His own eyes were beginning to get a little wet as well. It was like the future had suddenly opened up to him in that kiss, and all he saw was the amazing things that they would experience together. Their first Christmas. Planning the wedding. A kid, maybe two. Whatever it was, he couldn't wait.

"Here's to the happy couple!" Ben toasted.

Bart realized that he had his happy ending after all.

"I love you," Missy said, breaking the kiss once more to rest her forehead against his.

"And I love you," Bart said, meaning it more than he had ever meant anything in his entire life.

They held each other for quite a few moments, clinging to each other with more love and desire than they'd ever had.

And Bart knew, with no uncertainty, that he would continue to love her for the rest of his life.

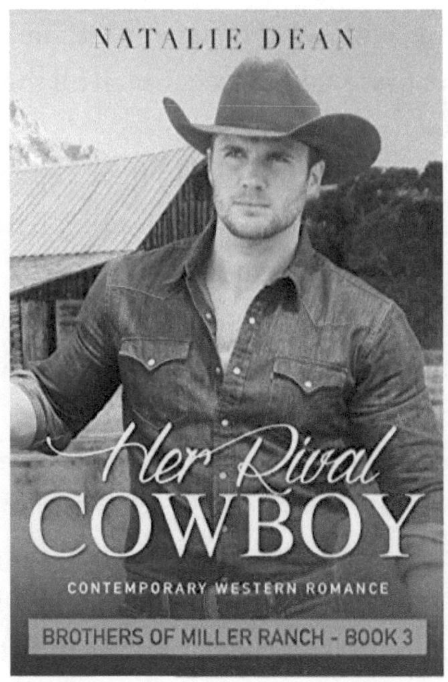

HELLO READER! I hope you enjoyed Saving her Cowboy. Up next in the Brothers of Miller Ranch is Benji and Danielle's story. Ma asks Benji if he can go help out on the neighbor ranch, but when he gets there, Dani (short for Danielle) is less than enthusiastic about his presence. She's a tomboy through and through who loves working with the animals but would rather keep to herself. She's nothing but suspicious of the handsome cowboy from the rival ranch next door.

You can find Benji and Dani's story on all major retailers. Plus, you can find it on my own online bookstore if you'd like to support my small mom-owned business. I'd be honored if you chose to do so. Scan the QR code below to be taken to Her Rival Cowboy at Natalie Dean Books. If scanning QR codes isn't your thing, you can also find my store here: nataliedeanbooks.com

ABOUT THE AUTHOR

Born and raised in a small coastal town in the south, I was raised to treasure family and love the Lord. I'm a dedicated home-schooling mom who loves to travel and spend time with my growing-up-too-fast son.

When I'm not busy writing or running my business, you can find me cleaning house, cooking dinner, feeding our three rescue cats, trying to make learning fun and coaxing my son to pick up his toys. On less busy days, you may also find me paddling down a spring run in Florida, hiking a mountain trail in Georgia (on the rare vacation to the mountains), or enjoying a book.

If you love Natalie Dean books, you can be notified of new releases by signing up to my newsletter at nataliedeanau thor.com, where you will also receive two free short stories for signing up. Just click on the "Free Books" tab at the top and you'll be on your way!

Also, as previously mentioned, I've opened my own online bookstore and I'd love your support! As of June 2024, I'm selling my ebooks at Natalie Dean Books. By late summer or fall 2024, I should have audiobooks, regular paperbacks, large print paper-backs, dyslexic print paperbacks and signed paperbacks all available. At the request of my loyal readers, I'll also be adding merchandise, such as glasses, cups, magnets and more. So come check out my small mom-owned author business at nataliedean books.com.

You can also scan the QR code below to be taken to the home page of Natalie Dean Books.

facebook.com/nataliedeanromance